DUMP

AND

CHASE

Jennifer,
May all your dreams
come true.
Fellow Cleve Hiller
Joe Custodi
11-23-18

Joe Custodi

For more information, email joecustodi564@gmail.com

ISBN: 979-8-88759-992-2 - paperback
ISBN: 979-8-88759-993-9 - ebook

This book is dedicated to the survivors of Hurricane Ian in 2022.

This book is a work of fiction. Any resemblance to events or characters living and dead are purely coincidental.

Contents

1

H ere in Florida, when you live here, the first question when you meet someone, is invariably, "Where are you from originally?"

My name is Joe, Joe from Buffalo. I was living in my buddy's basement, no heat, in winter, in Buffalo, for God's sakes. How did I get here, what happened? How did I get to this low point, both figuratively and literally? Oh sure, I am a hearty native, lived here most of my life, put up with the long, extensive winters, the frozen lakes, and ponds for almost 50 years, and what did I have to show for it? Lifelong friendships were made here, got married here, had kids here, but I don't know anything else, so I guess it is what it is. Just accept your fate and miserable condition, self-effacing in my frigid, unyielding universe known as home. Even after all this time away, I still have the audacity to call it home, go figure?

Now, my folks on the other hand, they not only had time and the resources to pretty much live anywhere they could, yet they choose to live here, but not me, never wanted to look back when I punch my ticket and say, "Gee, I wonder what if....?" We all choose our destinies. Whether they quite work out the way we dreamed they would, or implode like a Supernova in the universe, well, how we react to it, pick ourselves up from failures, that's on us. I have an aunt that was even better off and more settled than the folks, yet she has lived in the same house she grew up in, since 1953! We even have pictures from when I was a kid of five years old, and the same exact furniture and decorations remain in place to this day.

Oh, and I have an ex that is always up my ass about how I screwed up our lives and three kids I barely know anything about, except for what they want on birthdays and Xmas. Friends have come and gone, most have moved on with their lives to separate phases, so where does that leave poor little Joey?

Oh sure, I have that glamorous, stable gas station attendant job at one of those nameless large box store chains that offers discount gas prices to its EXCLUSIVE members. If some of these members just drove about two miles to the next town over, they'd find cheaper gas prices. 'Guaranteed lowest price within 10 miles, or we refund the difference', my ass. What idiots, what are we, two cents lower per gallon, who would drive around for that? Oh wait, I would, I suppose. The only saving grace was the pizza delivery job off the books for extra cash to help me enjoy the finer things in life, like the ice-cold draft at the local watering hole. So, why am I constantly fucking up and getting kicked out of places or voluntarily moving to new ones to be happier? My habits, which usually revolve around drinking draft beers and eating cheap chicken wings at any local tavern, either with my brother or any "friend of the day" willing to listen to my woes or past hallucinatory successes I thought I had.

So, here I am, no money, no savings, no future plans other than the weekly Friday fish fry at any local place that "serves the best fish fry in town". Of course, there are about fifty such places that claim that lofty designation. I wonder if the folks over in Sloan know about the best place in Tonawanda. So here I am in my friend Joel's basement that he set up as a bedroom for me, only charging me about three hundred bucks a month, everything included. He held back the fact that I would share said basement with his son who had a private room. The only good part of it was he banged different broads constantly, so at least there was that pleasant diversion at times. Hey, what can I say, some of the broads were hot. Add to that fact there was only one bathroom on the main floor. Of course, when his mom, stepdad, girlfriend, son and whatever floozy he had were all there, the line to the shitter was like a line at the amusement park. What's a guy to do for privacy?

One day, I am laughing hysterically like a banshee for no apparent reason. "Joe, why are you laughing like that?"

"Joel, I can't be any lower than this, living in someone's basement in winter."

" It could be worse, Joe, you could be living with your batshit crazy sister-in-law and brother, or your lonely overbearing aunt. What's so bad about it?"

"Call me pessimistic by nature or selfish, but I don't know man, I need something more than this, maybe a place where I don't see my breath when I am in my room."

"Maybe your boss at the pizzeria will let you stay with him till you get on your feet?"

"That would be awkward considering I am banging his daughter in law on the side. He might not appreciate her sneaking in and out of my bedroom window like that."

"Yeah, that could be awkward, agreed. So, what are you going to do, just pack up everything in January and drive down to Florida on a whim? You sound like a guy that just got out of college with a liberal arts degree with no plan, no direction, no idea what to do next."

"What have I got to lose, Joel? I have decided I am leaving in January for warmer places unknown, somewhere in hot and sunny Florida, I can't take it no more."

"Hey Paul, Joe here thinks he is just going to get in his car and drive down to Florida, maybe they have a spot for me there."

"Where did you say Joe was going again, Joel?"

"He says he is going to Florida, Paul. He will be back like the lost cat."

"Yeah Joel, but he will be like a declawed cat, and has the awareness of a potato, and that's giving the potato more credit than it deserves!"

"Well, Joel and Paul, the nameless large retail box store chain has locations there, maybe they will transfer me, and I am sure there are pizza places too. I can deliver, see you around."

So, I made up my mind, going to a place I never even visited, not knowing a soul, not knowing what I would be getting into. I packed up my stuff into my minivan, yeah, I know, creepy middle-aged man with a minivan, but again, story for another time. So here I am, mid-January, minivan packed and ready to go with all my worldly possessions, no need for a moving truck, or a van, hell, not even a cart attached to the back of the vehicle. Sad part is, even though the van was filled, I would have had room for a traveling companion.

2

Joe

Hometown: Buffalo, NY

Age 50

Caucasian Male

5'5" on tall day, 170 pounds, brown hair, blue eyes

Divorced

Part time gas station booth attendant

Buffalo Sabres hockey fan

Qualities:

Drunk all the time.

Life of the party

Gullible

Always in the wrong place at the wrong time

Sexually Confused

Highlights:

Drinks Budweiser Drafts

80's Cheese music fan, especially Whip it by Devo

Favorably compared to Paul Lynde from Hollywood Squares

Once groped Barbra Streisand in an elevator in Chicago thinking it was Brittany Spears

Wears women's underwear claiming it adds to seduction of women (kinda faggy, you ask me)

Once sat next to a gaseous Rosie O'Donnell on a flight from NY to LA

Todd

Hometown: Cincinnati, OH

Age: 45

5'9", 210 pounds, stocky, brown hair, brown eyes

Single, never married

Works in medical supply field

Rangers fan

Qualities:

Whines about his job

always tired from lengthy bike rides

Knows where every happy hour is within 20-mile radius

Drinks Budweiser drafts but prefers a good Cosmo every so often.

Highlights:

Donated to the "Save the Communist dictator" fund and now on every mailing list known to subversive governments.

Loves rap music, especially Lil Wayne and Drake

Thinks Michael Jackson was severely underrated.

Cliff dove off the Cliffs of Dover in Ireland

Rode his bike into the Pacific Ocean when distracted by a mutant seal.

Once stiffed on a date by Whitney Houston who went out with a guy named Bobby Brown (we know how that turned out)

Likes puppies and anything cuddly.

Rick

Hometown: Detroit, MI

Age: 60

5'9", 200 pounds, silver and black hair, moustache, hazel eyes Caucasian male

Divorced

Retired, working on building his own home.

Red Wings fan

Qualities:

Forgetful

Always late

Likes Yuengling Light, but prefers Canadian beer (not available in most locations in Florida currently)

Highlights:

preference for strippers and hoes

Once dated Zsa Zsa Gabor thinking he would get all her money

Door's fan thinks Jim Morrison is alive on a beach in South Africa

Once detained at the Canadian Border trying to smuggle sand from the Hudson Bay into the States

Picked up a then struggling girl on his way to Toronto who went on to become Queen of England and had that very road named after her

Jeremiah

Hometown: Washington, DC

Age: 30

6'1", 250 pounds, red hair, green eyes

Caucasian male

Single (unhappily)

"Pharmaceutical sales rep" works for the syndicate.

Flyers fan (what is with these guys following teams from other cities?)

Once took the Taco Bell chihuahua on a cross country trip

Qualities: Drinks anything wet and cold

Eats like a horse.

Highlights:

Heads the "save the whales" campaign in Yucatan, Mexico, and parts unknown in South America

Likes techno music, especially with electric harmonicas.

Completed the triathlon in Hawaii only to discover he did it in the wrong order.

Played goaltender for the girl's field hockey team when half of the men's lacrosse team had to fold when a rare hoof and mouth disease resulted from a steak dinner at the Golden Corral

Once had a torrid love affair with singer Stevie Nicks

Tung Hang Low

Hometown: Nagasaki, Japan

Age: 25

5'4", 130 pounds, brown hair, slanted eyes

Half Japanese, partly Samoan, Indian, with a mix of Alaskan Eskimo and Swedish

Marital Status: Undetermined as of this writing

Comic relief

Charleston Chiefs fan from movie Slap Shot

Qualities:

Drinks sake' but prefers Colt 45

Loves reggae music and worships Bob Marley

Shares a fetish with Joe.

Highlights:

Totally fictional made-up character to make the story more interesting.

David

Hometown: Philadelphia, PA

Age: 40

6'6", 300 plus pounds, blue eyes, balding

Caucasian male

Single

Homebody

Cowboys fan (another one rooting for team from another town)

Qualities:

Chronic pot smoker extraordinaire

Drinks expensive bourbons but occasionally likes a good tango

Collects celebrity potato chips

Highlights:

Once consumed a barrel of pickle juice and peed green for a week straight.

Missed patenting the pet rock by exactly one day and did not receive any royalties whatsoever.

3

I don't know how I, of all people, got to this point. I was single, well, divorced, actually. When do people that are divorced call themselves single again, a day, a month, five years after the divorce?

I was waiting outside the dilapidated, desolate house for my "girlfriend" Stephanie. I'm really not sure what to call her, my companion in crime, my parasitic paramour, occasional concubine, companion? The house was located on the lower East Side of Buffalo, the type of block where the houses had been razed. Now, most of the empty plots serve as small urban gardens where tomatoes, cucumbers beans and squash are grown. The house we stopped by had electric extension cords reaching it by nearby houses. Clever way to save on your electric bill, I thought.

As with most modern relationships, ours was an on again off again thing, a work in progress. It was mostly off when she would disappear for weeks on end, and again, when she would come crawling back, usually extremely late at night. I would hear this little knock on the door, my name called out softly in a sweet, hushed tone. "Joe, Joe, aren't you going to let me in so we can have a little fun?" All of a sudden, I'd hear myself in an impulsive, irrational voice, "why, why, why?" Why does she keep showing up, I can't get rid of this chick. It can only be one thing that drives me or is it another reason too? That I am helping her beat her destructive tendencies and habits. She is a total knockout, a genuine head turner. When we are out in public, I see many looking over at us, or honestly, at her mostly, probably wondering what she is doing with this short potbellied, balding yet decent looking guy? I guess it plays to my ego, "yeah, tough guy, she is here with me, jealous much?" But if they only knew what hell I'd been through, they'd turn and run away screaming, maybe even move out of the area completely. Oh sure, she was a modern-day Aphrodite but to say she was a hot mess would be an under exaggeration of the magnitude kind. On top of her many quirky habits, including but not limited to her preference of eating pink colored Playskool brand chalk, not the usual chalk the teachers used for chalkboards at school. She had a ginormous appetite for 40+ oxycontin pills daily, usually 5 mg or more. Sometimes she would add a couple hits of crack to her repertoire to calm herself down. So here we are on one of our "dates", our date being defined as stop bys at drug houses on the lower East side in search of said drugs. I guess I always went along because it was better than sitting at my place alone all the time, as if being out and about with her was an active lifestyle, getting something done in my mind. Still, this was my life as it was, I didn't mind, it was something to do something to keep me believing I had a real relationship, finally.

I was sitting in my car in a daze of sorts when Stephanie came sprinting from the back right side of the house. I was parked in the front a few doors down, to be inconspicuous. What I forget to mention in this recall of events of that tragic day is that my vehicle is a 1979 Yellow Chamois 3 door hatchback Pinto with woodgrain paneling. She grabs the side of the door, dives into the front seat, her head landing between my legs.

"Oh, are you in the mood right now, I ask?"

She screams, "no, I am not in the mood, let's get the 'F' out of here!"

"What's wrong, what happened, Stephanie?"

Stephanie blurts out," I thought I was the only one there with my friends, Joe but there was another girl in a back room. I could hear her whimpering; I heard her cry out then it got quiet. I was coming out of the bathroom down the hall, the door was cracked open just a bit, but I saw this dark-skinned behemoth of a man look over at me, and his hands were wrapped around her neck, it looked as if she went limp. He looked up and started coming out the door at me when he saw me. I booked as fast as I could, holy shit, holy shit, holy shit."

Joe peeled out of his spot and fled the scene. Joe was thinking, how could others not have noticed him over these past few months of trips to the seedy area. As usual, Joe's blaming others for his own predicaments.

"What have you done Stephanie?" I am so screwed, I never got into trouble, never even got pulled over by a cop for a traffic stop. So, ok, there was that one time at the border crossing involving the harmless oversight regarding some produce being transported over international boundaries, but it was dismissed readily." How did I get in this pickle, Joe wonders? He was thinking how he'd always thought his life was hum drum, totally boresville, nerdsville even, as Stephanie always used to say.

A few weeks later, there is a headline prominently displayed across the front of the hometown newspaper- "Unidentified white female, approximate age 20, found stuffed in a garbage tote and left along a vacant field on the east side. It is believed she was left there for about three weeks and was found when a pack of homeless dogs were fighting over what were described as putrid meat pieces. A strange looking vehicle was last seen leaving that area at about that time and whereabouts, though one of the witnesses said it was the stupidest vehicle he had ever seen. If anyone knows the whereabouts of the vehicle described, please call the tipline at 555-Help".

Joe shakes his head in disbelief as he reads the article. He thinks aloud, "How did I get involved in all this? Should I just let it play out or should I come forward and tell the police what I saw that day?" Though, in all honesty, he only briefly glimpsed the huge monstrous guy that day he sped off with Stephanie. "If I did contact the police, would I even be safe?"

Now, he starts to get paranoid. Luckily, he was living in his buddy's basement in the suburbs and was able to leave the noticeable car parked behind his buddy's garage, out of sight. Luckily, he could bus to his job downtown and walk to the local taverns for his nightly dose of stress relief. He hadn't seen Stephanie since that night and did not want to get involved but he felt he couldn't stick around town and tell the police what he saw that night. A sudden flash of insight also hit him, 'what if the guys that were at that house were out looking for him'?

The next day, he was resting on his makeshift bed in the dank, damp, poorly lit makeshift bedroom in the basement. The news was about a suspicious vehicle that was narrowed down to 1970-1979 Pintos, how many can there be in the whole area, much less the Chamois colored one he owned? How long till someone notices and the police come knocking? Worse yet, what if those thugs came looking for him to shut him up permanently? He had heard how other witnesses are silenced or disappear. He's not ready to be silenced, he has so much to live for, he thinks. Still haven't seen or heard from Stephanie either. He's hoping she just goes away once and for all.

Joe thought to himself, I can't live in this God forsaken basement forever though, Lord knows my life is in complete shambles. Maybe I need a new start, preferably somewhere new and far away, but where to go?

Joel could see Joe was stressed, and put together a few things, coming to the conclusion that it was Joe the police were looking for. He did not need the attention either and had a few possible options to help his friend. He had a 1985 minivan, silver, with wood grain paneling.

He could swap it with Joe, have the car wrecked and put it out of its misery. In addition to that, he had a connection in Fort Myers, FL, his crazy ex-wife's sister in-law that had lived there for a bunch of years, but in Joel's mind, getting his friend Joe out of the area, even if it meant sending him to this whacko's place, meant Joe was out of his hair. He took Joe aside one day and explained his solution to Joe and Joe was all too eager to take his offer. It was January, in Buffalo, for God's sakes, who wouldn't want to relocate to a much warmer, pleasant surrounding?

4

Some people come to Florida for the weather, some come to get a new start, some come for fame, some come to relax, some come to recover, some even come to run away from something, but you can't run away from yourself, you still are who you are. No matter where you are. Life is about having experiences, as long as no one gets hurt, why not have some fun along the way, right?

Like many stories, this story starts in a bar, a place called The Goal Crease, just off downtown Fort Myers in Southwest Florida.

As with any bar, Southwest Florida has its full-time regulars, the types that you can count on to be there all the time, then there are those who enter for one drink, never to be seen again. But just because they were only there for a short time doesn't mean they did not make their mark in some way, like a petrified bug's imprint found millions of years later when some construction guy stumbles upon an otherwise unnoticed hunk of rock that has been treaded on for millions of years and is still there. We all have our reasons for moving down here, some do, just to get away from the weather, some do it for a new job, some do it to run away from something, but we all have our reason for deciding that this is the place we choose to be and therefore, we have to make the best of it, good or bad.

This is a story about a highly unlikely pairing of a few odd characters that have something in common and is just as unlikely as the fossilized imprint. Their common threads being drinking beer, especially at The Goal Crease, home of the dollar draft and gator bites. The other common interest for their friendship, being their unusual passion for the sport of hockey. Not that the passion for hockey in and of itself is unusual, but passion for the sport in Southwest Florida where the beaches are open for business all year round is dedication of a morbid sort. Then again, as one of the guys written about in this book, Rick, likes to say, "Can you beat this?"

Why does everything have to make sense, and have a purpose? Can't we just enjoy each other's company along the journey in a random, spontaneous way, sometimes? Hockey is like life, there are faceoffs, penalties, goals, intermissions, and timeouts but eventually someone comes out on top.

Oh, by the way, for the most part, the names have not been changed to protect the innocent, nor am I liable for such follies committed in this book.

5

I had never met Joel's crazy ex-wife or her sister, nor had even spoken to her by phone till I was on my way. Joel gave me her number and told me that he had spoken briefly to her about me and vouched for my sanity and, more importantly, my ability to pay my share of the rent. She was down on her luck, I guess. Her ex pulled out of the place on a whim when he decided to join the foreign legion as a priest.

Why does everybody these days have exes? Joe didn't need to be in anyone else's drama, but he did need a place to stay so he was willing to take that chance. Halfway down there, he got on the phone to let her know he was on his way, that he would be there in a couple days. She hesitated on the phone and told Joe she was not sure he could stay there now, that her ex, though he was out of the country, might not be thrilled that a strange guy was going to stay with her. Joe got forceful and insisted he was on his way, no turning back, that a promise is a promise, where he comes from. They could deal with any issues or uncertainty after he gets there. Joe hung up and continued his route southbound. Little did he know what was in store for him in Fort Myers, but he was on his way, no turning back now.

6

Joe left Buffalo just in the nick of time, ahead of a nasty snowstorm. The storm pretty much followed him South and he was concerned about how the vehicle would hold up but eventually he made his way to Fort Myers. On the way there, he was in constant contact with Joel's crazy ex sis in law. Joe had first hand experience of her mental stability when she kept changing her mind as Joe was updating her about his eventual arrival, Joe even wondering if he had a place to stay when he arrived. His funds were limited and he could not afford to rent a motel room long term, maybe he would be immediately homeless upon his arrival? Finally, Kim relented about her doubts whether or not to let joe stay there. She realized that the rent she would charge Joe would more than cover her share plus a little extra something for luxuries like food and power.

Joe arrived on a beautiful January day and settled into his new digs more comfortably than he thought he might, although the 4 dogs inside and the one that was leashed to the doghouse in the disgusting outside yard might disagree with that.

The first few days there, Joe drove around to find where work, stores and the usual were located. A few nights after, he finally loosened up and treated himself to a few beers at a local place. When he walked in, he was obviously in the minority and the place grew quiet, but Joe being Joe, ordered a few and talked to the others and was given advice and instructions where to go and where not to go. Funny, he thought after, no one mentioned the place they were in, as a place to go, or not to go. He maybe had a few more than he should have but was glad what he learned so early in his tenure here in Fort Myers.

Joe was so thrilled to be in this place, even though he woke up hungover. Joe walked over with a case of Natural Ice to introduce himself to the neighbors. He had noticed the first few days as he was settling in that the neighbors were outside sitting on their front porch all day and night, rather, a poor excuse for a porch where chairs were arranged in a line by the front door. He had met so many people last night and found that they all compete voraciously for a free beer, or two, or more. Once, when Joe got up to use the bathroom back at his place and refresh the case after everyone consumed it in less than an hour, one of the guys, Juan, followed him back to help him get the new beers. How neighborly, Joe thought, until Juan told him that everyone at the party was a bunch of drunks and will continue drinking the beers until they are all gone. But Joe wanted to fit in, so he didn't mind, a couple cases of beer to make new friends and possible allies was worth it, he thought. Later, when Juan got up and left,

Sammy, the dark skinned elder, and apparent leader of this gang, spoke up and told Joe to not trust Juan and that he will only pretend to be friendly to get as many beers as he could, that he was actually prejudiced and despised most white people. "Who to trust", Joe thought? After about two cases of beer were polished off, Joe was dismissed quickly as a stranger would be, the party dispersed when they ran out of beer.

Joe was still a little woozy from the night before. What do they put in that Natural Ice? He wondered what alcohol content was in them, as he felt his head throbbing unlike ever before. Joe was laying zombielike in his bed when he heard a frantic loud knocking at his door. He gets just enough energy to pull himself up from the bed and stagger over to the door, peeks out the little makeshift eye hole, pulls the chain off the hook, unlocks the bolt, and sees Sammy from the night before. Sammy was perky and said he was glad to have met Joe, that the neighborhood needed some fresh blood, but that Joe being white and different from the others, that he might consider moving out? Sammy proceeded to tell Joe that in his daily observances of the immediate area and speaking to others that passed by, one guy asked where he, Joe, lived? The guy told Sammy he was a friend from his hometown and wanted to say hi to Joe, but Sammy held firm and told the man he did not see any white, middle aged, balding white guys around.

Sammy felt the hairs on his neck rise and sensed something was up with this well dressed, professionally clothed guy with dark glasses and a fresh, clean-shaven look. "Joe, I don't know what you did, or where you are from, or what you're hiding, that's none of my business, young man, but folks around here like their privacy and don't need no unwanted attention, you understand?

How about we have another beer and another chat, what you say?"

"Sammy, you seem like a cool guy and everything, but I ran out of beer last night, and I have not even started moving yet."

"Ok, Joe, I see how it is, if you don't need my help, just tell me. I will tell that guy next time I see him creeping around, where you are, do you want that?"

Uh oh, Joe thought, here we go again. He became extremely uncomfortable and came to the conclusion that either he would stick around here and deal with this mysterious stranger, or worse, this beer drinking piranha next door. He could not afford a case or more of Natural Ice nightly, welcome to Paradise, right?

7

The next night was uneventful, and Joe dozed off at about 11:00 PM. It seemed to be a short while when suddenly, a loud banging on the front door followed by a loud yelling, "Police, let us in!"

Joe froze and thought he was dreaming. No one else got up to answer the door, and it was silent until a few minutes later and an even louder knock on his bedroom door jolted Joe, who sat up in his bed bewildered. Suddenly, a bright flashlight was shown into Joe's eyes, and Joe was shocked into the realization that this was truly happening, it was not some kind of alcohol induced dream.

"Sir, Sir, I need to see your identification immediately, and do not make any sudden movements."

Joe panics and struggles to find his wallet, finally getting out his license and the police officer sarcastically asked Joe if he just moved there and what he was doing there currently. Joe explains how he just moved there, and he did not even know anyone else there other than the woman who stayed in the back bedroom. The police seemed to believe Joe, and just as quickly left the place, the door broke and off the hinge.

Joe was freaked out and decided right then and there that he could not stay at this crazy place. Joe thought to himself about the coincidences these past few days.

8

In the short time Joe was staying in Fort Myers, his new roommate and landlord, Kim, was getting very used to having him around, and more so the cash rent paid before the rent due date. And, having the vehicle that was the only one in working drivable condition in the house so that Joe could run her to work, to the stores, to her boyfriends or just out. This was not the deal Joe expected when he moved down here, but Joe was away from my miserable life and situation back home. He couldn't stay where he was at and put her and the others at risk, and more importantly he could not afford to stay there on his own, because of gas and beer and other associated unforeseen expenses to live at this place Joe had to decide whether to stay or go. He hastily made his decision. He scoured the Craigslist ads for a new place. How bad could it be, he thought, how much worse could it get than where he was? Joe called a few places and even met a one-eyed guy with a nervous twitch so bad it made him feel a little uncomfortable. He had lived in many unusual places over the years and had many interesting experiences regarding those living arrangements, but he never got the sense that one of those roommates were a serial killer. Go figure, a serial killer in Florida, no, that would never happen.

Finally, Joe talked to a guy that sounded normal and he was also from New York, so Joe could relate to him, or so he thought. Unfortunately, he lived far out in a place called Lehigh Acres, east of where Joe currently lived, and far from civilization. The rent was suitable, and he was not around most of the time, but the isolation and downright distance from other houses and people in general made Joe tense. This was the type of area where home invasions are pretty routine. Even the roommate, who was an ex-marine, would leave his doors locked even during the day when he was home. No one was within one-fourth of a mile, what's he thinking Joe thought, that some homeless Mexican or minority would stop by to borrow a cup of sugar? Joe became disillusioned believing he was not out in the open as he was in Fort Myers, or was he?

9

Joe was not satisfied in the new place he had suddenly moved to. He had to drive almost 25 miles to get to work and back and that cut into his time for enjoying his beer after work, so the one day he was off and decided to look around where he worked to find out if there were any little places that he could frequent. Translation, a dive bar that offered cheap drafts. He was driving along and out of the corner of his eye spots a little digital sign offering $1 Bud drafts all day! His vehicle literally screeches in front of the little place, he pulls into the parking lot and goes to the back where there is what looks like a tiki type bar and he enters place and takes a seat at the bar.

First impressions sometimes are wrong, but maybe this one was right all along. The place was called The Goal Crease . The World Cup Soccer games were in full force, a total summer sport if there is any such sport. (My apologies to America's pastime). His first thought sitting here was, where did all these Mexicans come from? Furthermore, why is that guy sitting here in a full mesh NY Rangers jersey in an outdoor bar in Fort Myers in July? The temperature is almost 90 degrees, and it is so hot, it makes Joe sweat to see him sitting there in it.

So, Joe, being the sociable, inquisitive, sensitive type, asked, "Dude, what's with the Rangers jersey in July?"

The guy looks over at Joe and says, "I am a Rangers fan and that never ends no matter what time of the year it is."

Joe was taken aback at first and replied "Yeah, but the playoffs ended last month. Sorry to say, your team lost, pal".

"I know, but they should've won, and I support them no matter what."

"Well, I am a Sabres fan and we have not been to the playoffs since Obama was in office, so I can respect that I guess. My name is Joe, Joe from Buffalo, how are you?"

"My name is Todd; I am from Cincinnati but follow the Rangers."

"Wait, you are from there yet follow the Rangers, whatever floats your boat, buddy."

"Well, I like the Columbus Blue Jackets too, and even had season tickets their first few seasons."

"Ah, so you're a turncoat, are ya?"

Todd seems thrown off, and scratches his chin, "huh?"

Joe thinks he was being witty but backs off, "never mind, but yeah, I like the Rangers behind my Sabres."

"Good for you, Joe, but at least my team has won the Cup in our lifetime."

"Well, at least I root for a team from the city I was born in, you should root for a team that might win it, someday."

"Sorry for being a homer, Todd. Why don't you root for my Sabres? We need more fans."

"Nah, was there once, boring town, other than chicken wings, besides NY is more fun to visit."

"So, what brought you down here, Todd?"

"The weather, you?"

"Pussy, what else, Todd? So, Todd, are you here full time, or one of those snowbirds that goes back every April and comes back and annoys us every winter?"

"I am here all year round, hockey is a round year sport nowadays, what can I say?"

There is an awkward silence and pause as though the two ran out of things to say.

Todd pipes up, "How about those Reds?" Joe immediately picks up on his cue.

"Hockey to baseball, huh, well, it is summer, and baseball is in season."

"Yeah, Joe, baseball is cool, but nothing beats hockey in 90 plus degree heat." Todd muses, "I wonder if we could build an outdoor rink here, someday?"

"That would be cool, Todd, I sure have a lot of fond memories of playing on the pond and ice fishing at the same time."

Joe selectively remembers the one time he had success playing on the frozen pond. "I once slapped a frozen perch into the net and won the game in overtime. Mom didn't mind skinning it afterwards even though it was pretty roughed up."

Joe, having moved here recently has not ventured out much yet. "So, ok, Todd, other than hockey, what other sorts of things do you like to down here?"

"Not much to do down here in winter, in Florida, I don't know, watch hockey and drink dollar drafts, what else?"

"I heard someone say something about the great fishing."

"Yeah, being surrounded on three sides by water would make it seem like there are fish around, I suppose?"

"Yeah, this being an island and all, I'd say we have a lot of that around."

Joe looks perplexed and wonders if Todd knows his Florida geography. Joe puts his finger in the air and then pulls back. "I thought Florida was a peninsula surrounded on 3 sides by water?"

"No, I'm pretty sure it is an island, why do you think they named it Florida with an A on the end?"

"Oh, ok, that makes sense, I guess, what else is there to do here, though, Todd?"

"I guess if you are outdoorsy, you can bike. I own a bike and ride it everywhere down here, to work, the beach, pretty much everywhere I have to get to."

"Sounds like a lot of work to get around to me, no thanks, Todd."

"Suit yourself, but I save a ton of money not having to pay for a car, there's golfing too."

"Cool, I have a set of clubs I have been meaning to break out, do you golf, Todd?'

"No, I had clubs, but they don't fit on my bike so well."

"You drive a Harley or something?'

"No, a Schwinn."

Joe had thought Todd was joking about the bike thing before. "Wait, you ride around in this awful heat?"

"Good exercise, Joe, you should take it up sometime."

"I don't know, Todd, seems like it is like asking for a heat stroke."

"I have a kayak, too."

"Cool, I never did that, sounds fun."

"I haven't kayaked in a while, but I have a place I have been wanting to kayak to, interested, Joe?"

Joe does not have much else going on and would like to start doing some things to enjoy his time down here. "Sure, give me your number so I can call you and make plans."

"Sure...it's Brian Leetch, Harry Howell, Adam Graves, Eddie Giacomin, Rod Gilbert, Andy Bathgate, Mark Messier, and my fav of all time, Mike Richter.

Joe's mouth drops and he is not sure how to respond. "Huh, Todd, what was that again?"

"I always give out my phone number in code, using former NY Rangers' uniform numbers to show my loyalty to the team. It also roots out any fake fans who say they follow hockey, and then when they don't know the names of the players, I know we can't be friends."

Joe is amused and befuddled. "So, you decide who to be friends with based on the fact they know obscure players from the past?"

"Not just any players, Joe, Rangers players."

"Well, I guess I can be your friend, Todd, because believe it or not, I even know who Glenn Healey is for the '94 team that won the Cup".

Todd brightens up at the revelation that someone does seem to know the sport of hockey down here in Florida. "Yeah, backup to Richter, 10-12-2, 3.03 goals against, Joe."

Joe has minor doubts about it but has to know, "just one question, Todd, do they lock you up somewhere every night when you go home?"

10

Almost a week passed by since they had met when Todd calls Joe and lets him know that he was kayaking the next day, and that he, Todd, would even rent the kayak for him, so Joe being cheap, agrees to this activity though he admittedly is a little nervous to go out on open water.

Joe stops by Todd's to pick him up and barely fits Todd's kayak in the back, but it fits well enough for the back hatch to shut. Todd pre-arranged a rental for Joe at the place on Pine Island that they were going to launch from. Joe has never been in this area and is still unsure about going out but figures a new experience would be fun and different. They are at a small park on the tip of Pine Island overlooking the Pine Island Sound.

"So, where are we, Tom?"

"My name is Todd, Joe."

"Oh, you remind me of Tom Arnold, sorry."

"This is Pine Island, and we are going to take a short kayak trip over there."

Joe is still trying to get his bearings about where he is. "Why is this called, Pine Island, I don't see no pines here, and by there, where do you mean?"

Todd points off in the distance and Joe cannot even see any land or island anywhere in view.

"It's out there past those other islands, you can't see it from here, it's called Cabbage Key."

Joe, being naturally curious and inquisitive about anything new states, "you sure have some strange names for places here, like that river, what's it called, the Calloo-hatchee or something?"

"It's called the Caloosahatchee, it's an Indian name."

"Oh, I get that, I am from a town outside Buffalo called Cheektowaga, that's Indian too."

"That is interesting and fascinating, Joe. Are we going to get in the kayaks or are we going to talk about Indian names of places that end in vowels because I could talk about Tuscaloosa all day if you want."

Joe gazes at the kayak sitting on the ground at the edge of the water. "Sure, Todd, we can go, but how do I drive this thing, and where is the motor?"

Todd is getting a little impatient and does not feel as though he must teach Joe the fundamentals as if he is a little kid out his very first time in a kayak. "It is not motorized; these are paddles, and we paddle in the water to propel the boat."

Joe puts his right hand over his eyes and peers out over the body of open water. "All the way out there, how do we get back?" Joe thinks he has a revelation and slaps his head lightly. Oh, I get it, a ship comes out there and brings us back, right?"

"Um, no, Joe, we paddle back."

Joe is dismayed and concerned a little. "Are you sure I can't hitch a ride back, maybe tie a rope on the end of someone's boat like a dinghy?"

Todd is undeterred to do this kayak trip one way or the other. "We'll see, but that defeats the purpose of kayaking out there."

"I dunno, Todd, seems like a lot of effort to end up right back here after all is said and done, ok, let's go, I guess, I wanted to try it, so might as well do it since we're here."

Joe tentatively goes to sit down in the kayak. Todd agreed he would help Joe get started and push him out to the water. Joe is very unsettled. "So, ok, Todd, how do you use these paddles?"

Todd glares at Joe and shakes his head but makes a rowing motion to show Joe how to row it. "You put one on each side, like this, and row towards the way you want to go."

Joe gets settled into the kayak and Todd quickly pushes Joe into the water before he can change his mind. He slowly starts to row, but the paddles are not close to being in unison as they are being dragged and splashed in the water, so Joe's kayak goes in circles and no appreciable distance is achieved. Todd starts to row and make a beeline for the destination.

Finally, Joe exasperatedly figures out the technique to some degree and the kayak starts to go in a direction, but why is Todd going that way and Joe going a completely different way? Todd finally looks back and figures out Joe is lagging behind. Todd realizes this is not going to be an easy kayak to the destination, it is not going to be the leisurely, carefree day he planned, but he doubles back and patiently explains to Joe the intricacies of keeping the oars straight in the water, how deep to stroke and finally after what seemed like a very long time, Joe seems to get it.

The Sound is very calm and there are no waves or wind to speak of, so Todd feels they can still make it Cabbage Key in time to have lunch and a few beers and get back by sunset. They are making progress to the destination; it is a perfect day, but Joe keeps making complete loops around Todd as they advance to Cabbage Key.

Joe is getting anxious and nervous about the fact that it appears the land is still as far off as when he started. He screams across the Sound to Todd "why do I keep going in circles?"

"Just follow me, Joe." Geesh, why did I bring him?

Joe starts to get a handle on the rowing technique a bit but being inexperienced, has misjudged the currents horribly and he continues on. Things are going better, and they can see where they are headed when Joe's kayak ends up along mangroves on a small island between Pine Island Point and Cabbage Key.

Todd looks back at his struggling companion and wonders how Joe ends up in this one small mangrove on the way, there is no other tiny island even, how did he get there?

Joe is still talking incessantly, Todd just wants the adventure to end, and the sooner the better.

"Todd, what are these trees doing in the middle of this lake?"

"First of all, they are called mangroves, and this is called Pine Island Sound and empties into the Gulf of Mexico."

"I better not get caught in some drift or current and end up in the Gulf or something, this is a rental for 6 hours only and I am not paying extra." Joe can't move his kayak as hard as he tries to straighten it and go in the direction of the open water, not bumping along the mangrove section of the island. "So, ok, Todd, if these are mangroves, and they are out in the middle of the Sound, why do I keep steering into them, I keep getting stuck in these trees, you'd think I could be away from them?"

Todd works his way behind to where Joe is. "Here, pull my paddle and I will get you "Here there."

"Gee, Todd, that sounds kind of personal, we are not even dating yet. How much further to this Cabbage Island?"

Todd points to a sliver of an island barely in sight. "It is called Cabbage Key, and not much further."

"That still looks pretty far to me, are you sure, how do you know which island is which, they all look alike to me."

"Just keep paddling, we will get a drink when we get there."

"A drink, huh, I like the sounds of that, Todd." Just then, the kayakers come to a spot where the channel is open, exposing them to speedy motorboats.

"Oh, by the way, Joe, you need to paddle faster through this part because boats come through this channel, and they do not always see kayaks."

Joe wants to call it quits and get back to land. "This is too dangerous; can I turn back?"

"We're almost there, little buddy, and there is cold beer waiting for us."

Joe perks up at hearing about the reward for this God-awful effort. "Cool, I like beer."

Suddenly, Joe glimpses what appears to be a very large fish jumping out of the water near to his kayak, in the process, splashing Joe. "What was that, Todd?"

Todd looks over unfazed by the sight of jumping fish suddenly. He does not want to freak Joe out any more than he already appears. "Those would be fish, Joe, this is a body of water."

Joe is terrified. "That one looked pretty damn big; how do they get here? Why are all these fish ahead jumping out of the water?" Just then, a tarpon lands squarely in the kayak and Joe panics and screams out. "Hey, one landed in my kayak! Get it out of here, Todd, aaahhhhh!"

Todd realizes Joe is in over his head with this last turn of events, so he paddles over closer. "Do you need help, Joe?"

The panic stricken, flopping fish leaps out of Joe's boat only to land unluckily in a larger fish' open, waiting mouth. "No, it flopped out on its own, but he didn't get very far, a bigger one came by and snapped him right out of midair, talk about bad timing. Are we almost there yet?"

"Almost, Joe." They are drifting along and come close to another island that Joe does not even notice when a small wave caused by a large, motorized yacht goes by and laps up on the side of Joe's kayak, causing the kayak to bob up and down and flip.

Joe is temporarily plunged under the surface until it flips itself over, Joe falling out of the kayak, splashing frantically. "Help, I'm drowning, the kayak flipped, help!"

"Calm down, Joe, you'll be ok, the shore is right behind you, put your feet down, you're in two feet of water here, relax."

Joe gets his sense of balance and finally feels the bottom of the shallow sound and is relieved as he is only about knee high in the water. "I thought I was going to drown," he says in a high pitched, shrieky yelp. Joe looks over at the passengers on the yacht that caused his kayak to capsize, pointing at him, laughing.

Todd pulls up as close as he can and sees that Joe is ok. "You're ok, unfortunately."

Joe is dripping wet, but now determined to get to that Key or whatever to get his reward of cold suds and conch fritters, as promised.

Todd assists Joe in getting back into the kayak. He holds his kayak in place while Joe gets strapped in again, and they finally arrive at their destination. Normally, Todd has made the trip in half an hour, this trip is about two hours and counting. Beer time has been severely limited, but Todd is determined to make the most of this disastrous trip.

Finally, they get to their destination and get on land. Joe drops to his knees and kisses the land as a long-lost sailor at sea would after being out on the open water for months and months, not minutes and minutes like Joe had experienced. Joe gets up, brushes the sand off his legs and feet and spots the little restaurant, as advertised.

"Now I'm wet too, damn. Speaking of wet, where's the beer? So, does this place have a restroom or I am going to go behind those trees?"

"Yes, there is a little restaurant over there, see?" Todd points at it.

Joe is befuddled. "Why did they put a restaurant way over here, seems like a stupid place for a restaurant."

"It's a tourist thing, they do not even have electricity here."

"How do the lights work then?"

"Powered by woodfire, I suppose?"

"How do they keep the beer cold?" Joe insists.

"Would you stop asking stupid questions?"

They head inside and Joe excuses himself to use the restroom, he is gone awhile but gets a seat next to Todd at the bar, when he notices the decorum of the establishment.

"Hey, Todd, look at all the dollar bills stuck up on the walls, I bet there are a million of them, we could be rich if we took them."

"Good luck with that, Joe, what are you going to do, tuck them into your kayak and paddle back unnoticed?"

"Humm, I did not think that part through, maybe next time?"

The place is starting to fill in, and a couple sit down next to them. Joe, being the friendly, gregarious guy he is, tries to initiate a friendly chat with the otherwise preoccupied couple. "So where are you folks from?"

"We are from Boston, you?"

"Buffalo."

"Oh, sorry to hear that."

Joe is taken aback by the comment but continues anyway. "Huh? Why do you say that? I like to say I am proud to be where I am from, but glad to be where I am."

Joe needed to figure out a way to get back without having to do all that exhausting paddling, he knew he would be even more tired than he was getting out of here. "How did you folks get out here?"

The couple shares a quick glance at each other in anticipation of this conversation not going anywhere productive or pleasant. "Um, boat, why?"

"Well, my friend Todd here is a pussy and we kayaked over here from way over there and he doesn't want to paddle back so he wanted me to ask you if we could ride back with you? I would paddle back, of course, but I have a date later and she might not be thrilled with me smelling like a fish. It's kinda hot in here too. " Joe makes a waving gesture under his sweaty armpits.

The gentleman looks worriedly over, shaking his head. "Sorry, pal, we aren't going back that way."

Joe is starting to get enraged; he just wants to get back to the starting point of this adventure. "Oh, you say you're not going back our way. You came from there, well, we'd be open to going back with you and you can drive us over to Pine Island from there, for Todd's sake, of course."

The man is not swayed in his thought that he was not going to take this twerp and friend anywhere and comes up with what he feels is an unassailable excuse. "We have to pick up our precious poodle at the poodle store after." The couple hastily settles their tab and leaves the immediate area.

Joe is left sitting at the bar speechless. They have to go now to pick up your poodle at the poodle store, Joe ponders. He turns to Todd, who is in a trance staring at the sports replay show on the TV. "Some people around here are not too friendly, you know, Todd, that's why they're called Massholes, I guess."

"You are scary, Joe, do you ever shut up? And what did you mean for Todd's sake, you are the pussy, not me. Let's get going before it gets dark or you might unexplainably, mysteriously suffer an accidental drowning. Last thing I need is to be up all night with the Coast Guard explaining how your kayak flipped and would not flip all the way back over."

They look around and Todd holds his hands out, but Joe does not want to paddle all the way back, he is feeling sore already. "Looks like everyone left already, we are the only ones here" Todd says. There must be someone to get a ride back with, ok, let's go, I guess".

The paddle back is even longer than the trip there, it seems as though land looks farther and farther than when they started, and Joe is beside himself, but he must keep going. Joe is exhausted now and starts to panic that he won't be able to make it back. In what he thinks is a universal SOS sign, he raises his paddle frantically at boaters going by, hoping one of them will see this action as a signal of distress and pick up Joe. To his dismay and astonishment, the few boats that go by not only do not slow down but wave and smile at Joe as if everything is fine and dandy. Joe notices there is some distance between he and Todd and screams out, "this is a longer trip back than coming out here, why does the land seem to be getting farther away as I row more, and why do you keep ending up far away from me, Todd?"

"I have my reasons, it's in case you have an accident, I can get to shore quicker to get help."

Even though it was physically grueling to kayak today, Joe was happy that he went. "Aww, thanks, it's nice to have good friends that care, thanks, Todd."

11

Todd's place is near The Goal Crease and is basically an oversized studio for way too much money in Joe's mind, but it is set up as Joe likes it, with sports banners and some cool chairs to view sports on TV.

"Nice place, Todd, what's the seat doing in here?"

"Oh, that's the seat I sit in to watch every Rangers game."

"It looks like a seat from a hockey arena, cool."

"Remember the old Montreal Forum?"

"Yeah, Todd, is this seat from there, did you buy this when they knocked the place down?"

"Well, I don't think bought is the term, I had it removed before the auction. Swiss knives come in handy at the darndest times, you'd be surprised. I have a special affection for this particular seat. I was in it when Guy Lafleur scored for the Rangers against his old team, the Canadiens."

"I'm thirsty, got any cold beverages, Todd? I could use a frosted mug for this beer." Joe brazenly goes through the fridge looking for a beverage or snack. He spots a frozen slice of pizza in the freezer. "What's this in your freezer?"

"Oh, that's a once bitten slice of pizza from Wayne Gretzky. I saw him eating it at Famous Ray's in downtown Manhattan, saw him throw it in the garbage, so I fished it out of the garbage and kept it as a keepsake from the greatest player, not many can say that what, he was with the Rangers at the time not the Kings."

"How long have you had that in the freezer?"

"Well, he played on the 96-99 squads, so, what, been awhile now?"

"You have issues, Todd. So, what's going on today?"

"I was going to go down to the beach, catch happy hour later, want to go?"

"Sure, I can drive you, want a ride?"

"No, I will bike down, I have to keep my shapely figure intact."

"I see. I will catch up with you down there."

Todd packs up, gets on his bike and heads down to the beach. Joe hangs out and has a cold beer and takes his time getting down there to meet Todd. As Joe is driving towards his secret spot to park free, he looks over at a man who appears to be flat on his back, a mangled bike next to him. No one has gone to help him and they leave him sitting there as though he is a homeless person just taking up space. Joe just then realizes it is Todd, so he drives to his parking spot and takes a little while to check up on Todd. He shakes Todd when he is standing over him to rouse him from his peaceful lumber.

"What happened to you, why are you bleeding like that?"

Todd groggily awakens, sits up slowly and brushes himself off.

"Darndest thing, Joe, I was right down the road here, and a car hit me on my bike!"

"How did that happen, Todd?"

"I was cruising along when a car with a group of Spring Breakers decided to switch lanes all of a sudden and go right, and I could not slow down and got banged on the side of their car."

"Are you ok?"

"I'm a little sore but yeah, I had to get to Happy Hour though."

"That is total commitment, I agree."

"Yeah, as I was laying here dazed and not feeling too good, young guys from the bar across the way yell out 'we like your shirt, go North Stars.'" Todd looks down at his retro Minnesota North Stars jersey.

Joe is impressed. "It is a pretty cool shirt."

Todd continues, "it was a big mess and the guys that hit me said they wanted to pay me for my troubles, but I told them, just buy me a beer and we'll call it even."

"Was it at least a Premium brand, bottled or draft?"

"Domestic draft."

"Cheapskates."

They get up from the site of the accident and head to the Happy Hour place that sells 99 cent drafts and $5 appetizers and act as if nothing happened earlier.

Joe wants to continue partying at the beach but wants to appear as if he's concerned for Todd.

"Do you want a ride back home?"

"Sure, just don't hit any bikers on the way home. I am glad you have this van to fit my bike in the back."

Joe does not offer to let his friend stay there and pick him up. Instead, they both walk back to the van, stopping to scrape the mangled bike off the sidewalk. It is laying there untouched. They start to drive back to Todd's place when Todd notices Joe's annoying habit of constantly honking his horn at other motorists.

"Joe, why did you honk your horn like that, no one is in front of us or cutting us off."

Joe toots his horn. "I know, I find that people here are pretty friendly and always honk their horn at me for some reason, so I toot back a friendly honk back at them.

Todd looks over at one car speeding by Joe and putting his middle finger up as he passes Joe.

"That guy is sticking his middle finger at you and cursing; I don't think that is too friendly."

Joe's tone and attitude changes. "Screw him, what's the rush anyway, this is Florida where everyone is supposed to be nice, and on vacation. Why does everyone have to rush everywhere? Some people have such bad manners."

Todd notices they have driven past his place. "Hey, Joe, you passed my place."

"No problem, I'll swing back." Joe is travelling in the right-hand lane and abruptly cuts across the left lane and the grass covered median of the four lane highway and makes a quick U-turn and starts back to the entrance of Todd's apartment complex.

"You're not supposed to do a U-turn here, what are you doing?"

"Relax, the Canadians do this all the time." Joe turns into the apartment complex and pulls into a spot near Todd's apartment. He gets out of the van and takes the damaged bike from the back and puts it on the ground and gets back in his van. He rolls the window down as Todd is exiting. "Well, I hope you feel better, sorry you were hurt."

"That's ok, Joe, the thing that ticked me off the most was that it cut into Happy Hour. Now that is a crime, you ask me."

12

J oe is off another day from his part time gas station attendant job and decides to go to the Goal Crease as usual. He notices an older guy staring aimlessly at the TV and decides to say hi. He notices the Detroit Red Wings game is on.

"OK, who watches the frigging Red Wings in here?"

"That would be me, partner, why?"

Joe is aggravated that this new guy he never saw before has the game on that he wants, unlike Joe who usually must watch what some other fan has asked the bartender to put on TV.

"It's just that I never see the Sabres on here. Everybody seems to be from somewhere else here. Where are you from, I suppose Denver, or somewhere other than Detroit?"

"No, Detroit, why? "

"I keep meeting folks from places that do not root for their hometown team. My name is Joe, Joe from Buffalo, you?"

"Rick, nice to meet, even though your team sucks."

"I would not mind going to the playoffs every year but what can you do, though you needed an ex-Sabre to win the cup for you, Hasek, so do you live here or just visiting?" Joe makes a gesture to the bartender, sees that Rick has money laying on the bar and gestures to take the money from Rick's pile. Rick notices the subtle gesture and puts his hand over the cash, leaving Joe to pay for his own round.

"Moved here, picked up a fixer upper over on Cape Coral, should be ready to move in by January."

"Cool, I heard there are some good deals over there. What do you do jobwise?"

"I am a retired seafood distributor, I supplied octopus for the Red Wings games that the fans throw on the ice after every goal and occasional away games. Winnipeg and Vancouver allowed it. We tried it in Phoenix, but the octopus would decay and smell. We had success at the old Igloo in Pittsburgh, but Penguins fans can be so elitist, so the idea never took off."

"How do you make a living doing that, you make that much from doing that?"

Rick toys around and in a matter-of-fact straight face answers Joe. "Oh, you'd be surprised how much squid you can make, especially if you reuse the same one over and over."

Joe squints at the comment. "I thought you said it was an octopus. So, do you do your business from here now, afraid there aren't too many ice rinks down here?"

"No, I sold the idea to a front from the Russian mafia when they decided to muscle in on the action. Sergei Federov, the ex-Red Wing is involved, nice guy, actually. Too bad the ruble is worthless; I would have done better."

"Where are you staying now if the house isn't ready?"

"I sleep in my truck at Coochie Ha-Has strip Club over on route 41 and slip back to my place to wash up, though not having running water kind of makes it difficult. Not having a roof or walls even during dry season can be challenging."

"Don't they mind you staying overnights on their lot like that?"

"No, I think management thinks it keeps a certain element away at nights, plus I get last shot at any of the desperate homeless strippers and hoes. You'd be surprised what kind of action a drunk middle-aged guy can get at closing time. Of course, I usually have to stop at the ATM every morning. Funny thing is, I can never remember what happened after the last drink."

"I could never fix up a place on my own."

"Yeah, it's hard work but I built my sister's tool shed so I thought I could take my knowledge from that project and apply it to my place, it shouldn't be too hard."

"So, what brought you down here in the first place, Rick?"

"I had to get away from that snitch."

Joe did not clearly hear what Rick said.

Huh? "

"I mean I had to get away from that bitch, the ex."

"Yeah, those ex's can be bitches, true."

13

Rick rented a place close by The Goal Crease and made it a nightly habit to stop by for refreshments after working on his place all day usually, and Joe had been going there daily pretty much, so they would see each other around, taunt each other about how bad their teams were. Rick had noticed Joe's habit of being distracted on his phone most of the time he would see Joe up there. He even played pranks by hiding the phone when Joe would leave it on the bar. In Joe's mind, his leaving the phone meant that he was saving his spot. Joe was letting his buddy Rick buy the rounds of $1 Bud drafts as he usually does when they are there.

Joe seems even more anxious and jerky than usual; Rick thinks to himself. Joe comes from the bathroom smiling and distracted. "Hey, Joe, I notice you texting a lot today, what's with that, is it another one of your women?"

"Kind of, Rick."

"What do you mean, kind of?"

"Oh, it's just someone I text with that I have never met in person, and probably never will. Wanna see what she looks like?" Joe pulls out his cell phone and proudly shows Rick the contents that he has accumulated over months. Rick skeptically looks at the cell phone, thinking Joe has been duped, but changes his mind when Joe hands over the phone for inspection.

"Sure, wow she is a knockout, Joe, how do you know she is real? I never trust a chick unless she can get up and dance on a pole right in front of me."

"Well, here's another 10 pictures of her."

Rick is curious about this phone thing; he prefers his women within reach and can't understand the obsession with online and cell phones but he must admit he is impressed by what he sees. "Look at those knockers, you should hook up with her if you can, so what do you text with her about?"

"All kinds of stuff, but we 'sext' mostly."

"Sext, what is that?"

"Talk about sex, what we would do to each other if we saw each other."

"That sounds kind of lame to me, Joe."

"This from the guy that goes to Coochie Ha- Has nightly and has a $400 a night habit. But it gets pretty hot, clean and not messy and all involved. It fills in those times Joey is ready for some action, especially when I am at my place with no one around."

"But I thought you just said you were texting her now, were you doing that sexting thing right here?"

"Yeah, that's why I use the bathroom as much as I do here at The Goal Crease."

"Damn, man, and I shake your hand all the time, makes me want to rethink that in the future."

14

Joe made up his mind to leave the place in Lehigh Acres once and for all, despite the fact he was kind of hidden away there. He had no real incidents or worries of people looking for him, though the police responded to a tripped alarm at the place and checked his ID and even suggested that he have it replaced with a Florida license. Unbeknownst to Joe, it was required by law to change your license. He lied to the officer and told him that he had just moved down to Florida a week ago and he would change it very soon even though he knew in his head that it would not happen.

He called the prospective landlord before their get together to finalize the details of the move, deposits, etc. Joe wanted to make the move as quickly as possible, so he packed most of his stuff in the van, most of that comprised in the couple drawers of clothes he owned, a few boxes and a clock radio and cooler. He pulled up to David's, the new landlord, and saw that David was not there, so he walked down the block to the bodega. Joe knew from past experience that a bodega was a great place to get a cheap quart. While he was away, David walked up his driveway and saw this very outdated silver van with woodgrain paneling. He was starting to have doubts about renting the room he had to a whacko with a van almost as old as he was. The guy, Joe, he had spoken to by phone, sounded reasonable and sane, but who knows? Just to be sure, he peeked inside the van, rifled through a few boxes of clothes laying out in view and came across women's panties. Oh, David thought, maybe this guy Joe is a swinger and gets chicks but what guy has that many pairs of them, he thought? Joe finally came back after having consumed the whole quart on the walk back, conveniently throwing the empty can in the vacant lot next door. He shakes David's hands confidently.

"Thanks for renting the place to me. I needed a place closer to work, and especially closer to The Goal Crease. I was out in Lehigh Acres, and it took too long to get back and forth, especially to work. Besides, I am a regular now, at The Goal Crease and they would miss me if I stopped showing up. It's nice to be loved. And as much as I am into the ladies, my main mistress is a golden, honey dame in a frosted glass. Besides, it was weird out there, looked like a lot of inbreeding going on around there. I just need a place to sack out, I am never around, you will see."

David is perplexed and feels this guy Joe talks too much, but his last roommate was a nightmare.

"Ok, 500 bucks includes everything, and you have your own bathroom too."

Joe looks incredibly pleased and grins, relieved he does not have to share the bathroom with this oaf. "Well, that's good because I have been known to destroy those, if you know what I mean. Good eating habits will do that."

David lowers his head and voice. "By the way, Joe, I don't rent to gay guys, sorry, just not my thing."

"Huh, what do you mean?"

"If you think this is going to be some sort of hookup, it ain't going to happen, I don't swing that way."

Joe is slightly miffed at the comment. "Why would you say that?"

"I don't know, just a vibe I get."

Joe goes into defensive mode; he loves the location near to his new favorite joint. "I don't understand, why does everyone think I'm gay? I'm an older male and divorced and even have 3 kids."

David is genuinely surprised. "Really, you would have never guessed."

"Yeah, really, want to see their pictures? Joe rips out his wallet and flips through it, papers falling out. "Oh wait, I don't have any, but wait, here are their phone numbers on my cell phone. You can call them and check. I love pussy, I am all about the pussy. There is no more he man than me, got it?"

"Ok, don't get your panties in a bunch."

Joe is mortified his dirty little secret is out and turns red faced. "Have you been going through my clothes, Dave?"

"Huh, Joe, why would I look through your clothes?"

"It's just that, well, ok since we are going to be roomies and all, and I will be doing laundry here, you were going to find out anyway."

David is starting to get nervous now. "What are you talking about?"

"I wear women's panties, granny's panties though, not those thongs or anything, those would be uncomfortable."

David is beside himself and he does not want a flaming gay guy to be his roommate but desperately needs the cash to keep his hobbies and interests intact. "You wear women's panties? You sure you are not gay?"

"Nope, it actually makes seduction of women that much better. When they take my pants off and see me in these, they are putty in my hands. You should try it, you might like it, yourself. Besides, they are comfy and absorb my pee better when I have accidents. That can be embarrassing, as you know. "

David is still not convinced but accepts Joe's explanation. "No, Joe, no, I don't."

Joe is about to finalize the agreement when he can't help but notice that the place is bare and not a stitch of furniture anywhere other than an old TV and one kitchen chair in the living room.

"So, where is the furniture, David?"

"I don't believe in furniture, it makes one soft, then people get lazy."

Joe mulls the thought of nowhere to sit and drink but then he realizes all he needs is a place to sleep and eat. "Good thing I brought my mattress to sit on. Oh, and I can use my small cooler as a table to eat at, that should work out well." A loud rooster crowing nearby surprises Joe and makes him jump a bit. "What's that sound, was that a rooster crowing?"

"Oh, it's just a rooster, he lives next door, he doesn't disturb anyone."

"A rooster here in the city? I have never heard of a rooster in a city atmosphere, that is crazy, man."

"And he lays eggs too, so we always have fresh eggs around."

"Wait, a rooster doesn't lay eggs, do they?"

"No silly, that would be ridiculous, don't you know anything about chickens? But there are cows within the city limits here, too.

"No way."

"Way."

Joe has grown up in an urban setting most of his life. His only interactions with animals of any kind were usually thinly sliced in a deli wrapper or wrapped on a styrofoam plate at the grocery store. He sees a few cows across the street in an abandoned field. "What are cows doing here, where do they stay?"

"Well, in terms of what they do, they sit around and eat grass and stay in fields usually."

Joe is incredulous and yet curious. "This place is nuts. I suppose you're going to tell me that pet alligators roam around too?"

"Actually, they do roam freely, mostly at golf courses and behind some apartment complexes. One over on a golf course around here never bothers anyone unless they poke around in the water and he is sitting there right under the surface. I'm afraid that has not always gone well. Shame about old Leo Murphy, the one-legged golfer. He's still an excellent putter."

Joe has hedged a subject he meant to ask David upfront. "I notice we are the only whites on the block, are there any problems with that?"

"Only at the first of the month, just kidding, no problem. I moved here because I don't want to be seen as a racist. Between you, me, and the wall, I get along pretty much with everyone except niggers, spics and queers. Jews are ok as long as they stick to themselves."

Joe is incredulous at what he thought he just heard. "Wait, you just said you're not racist and yet you just said the N word, I don't get that. We live on a street with so many."

"I know, but they got the best weed, and I like drinking quarts of cheap malt liquor, I blend right in here."

"David, you are a 6-foot, 6-inch bald white guy that weighs over 300 pounds, you would not blend in at an Aryan Convention much less this block."

David is busy rolling something on the kitchen counter.

"What are you doing there?"

Rolling a fattie, wanna hit?"

"No thanks, I stopped back in '87 when I was stoned and had an appearance by President John Tyler to plead with me to stop smoking or I would grow ungodly amounts of hair in my ears."

David is feeling a little buzzed now. "Isn't he dead?"

"And your point being? Anyway, ever since then, Joey has been in a pot free zone, but thanks."

"Well, I like it and smoke every day, it keeps me active, actually."

"I thought pot made you lazy and want to eat munchies all the time?"

"No, I actually get energized, I know, most get listless, but I get focused and concentrate better."

Joe ponders David's insight. "Maybe I will start up again, I am usually running around like a chicken with its head cut off. I am surprised I have not seen that going on here."

"I know we just met, but you do seem nervous and jerky, Joe."

"My boss used to say that that before I was nervous and jerky, now I am just a jerk, ha." Joe is about to ask David what the next step is, even though David seems to be a bit quirky himself, he feels ok about moving here, especially with how close it is to his new favorite bar.

"One last rule, Joe, no sleepovers. If I ain't getting any, you won't be either, unless you want to share her, and I only mean her, no dudes, got it? "David reaches out to shake hands with Joe to finalize the agreement. "Oh, by the way, did you have any quirks or pet peeves that I should know about?"

"No, David, other than leaving messes or dishes in the sink for days on end, I am pretty easy going, how about you?"

"Nope, I just like to sleep all day and do my thing at night. I do have a few unusual hobbies; I collect potato chips that look like celebrities."

"Wow that must be hard to keep them when you are hungry."

"That's why I told you, I keep them right here, so please don't eat them if you see them around."

15

Even though Joe moved hastily from Buffalo and did not tell the others why, he has made the effort to call his folks regularly. Part of this routine was to let them know he was ok, but a big part of it was to brag about how wonderfully warm and sunny it was there.

"Hey, mom, how's the weather there?"

"Not good, it's minus 30 here and we are cooped up all winter." Joe cuts her off immediately.

"It's 80 here, mom and sunny, I told you that you and dad should come down here in winter."

"We have a monthly card game we'd miss, that would be so disappointing, we play for pennies, not dollars, just for fun and get pretty snockered, besides we don't know anyone down there and it's boring there. We have been wondering why you moved there. Your aunt thinks it is because you are hiding who you are, that you are gay and don't want anyone to know."

"Yeah, mom, I moved down here to be with my gay African American lover."

"Oh, really, is it true what they say, is he big down there, I heard they are huge. I could use someone like that, your dad has been a little lackluster in that area lately." Joe is aghast and puts his hands over his ears and holds the phone away from himself.

"What, mom, no, no, no, la la la, I can't hear you, I don't need to hear that, I am into women, just because I wear women's panties occasionally doesn't mean I am gay. Oops, did I say that out loud?" The cat is out of the bag, but wait, he can use this to his advantage, he thinks.

"Women's panties???? Good lord, our son's a freak, Joe."

"Mom, no, actually it helps me get laid by chicks, I am not gay, I swear!"

"What kind of panties do you wear, I like pink lace see through ones with a bow on the front of them." Joe is repulsed by the image in his mind.

"TMI, mom, please don't tell me that, no, no, no, I can't hear you, blah blah, blah."

"I always knew you were a little light in the loafers, your dad is going to be so disappointed."

"Mom, I am not gay, I swear, look, what about the kids I had with the ex, isn't that proof enough?"

His mom remains unconvinced. "We have our doubts that they are yours especially after what you told me, what will the rest of the family say, this will be on the family 800 hotline, I will be so embarrassed."

"You don't have to tell the rest of the family, mom."

"It's too late, your dad already posted it on Facebook."

"I guess I'll never be able to show my face at the family reunions, huh?"

"Where did we go wrong, we gave you everything and even let you take dance lessons even though we thought it was kind of different. You looked cute in your ballerina outfit though you probably should have danced the male parts. And now we are really wondering why you took figure skating lessons instead of playing hockey. How could we have been so blind?"

"Mom, there was nothing queer about those things, like I said, I did them to meet chicks. While the other guys were playing he- man sports and trying to impress the girls, I was handling their crotches with grace and ease at age 12. It takes a lot of hard work and manipulation to get little Suzy to let me do that, but I did. It takes strength and grace to pirouette with an 80-pounder raised above your arms, admittedly though, that is when I discovered how comfy it was to wear the women's panties. I'll never forget how Tracy back in 6th grade looked at me in those."

"And I thought she was a nice girl, that little slut. So, do you have a group or club or something that all you sickos are in?"

"There are no chapters that advertise down here, why, do you know of one, mom?"

16

J oe does not seem his normal, annoying gregarious self-tonight, and Todd notices he is more jittery than he usually is, and he is quieter too. They were just here last night, and things seemed to take a turn for the better for Joe, by the looks of it. He was spotted talking eagerly with a very alluring lady that had not previously been seen at the bar. Joe and Todd, being as regular as a regular could be at the place, knew the comings and goings of almost everyone there.

"Hey, Joe how are you feeling after last night at The Goal Crease?"

"What do you mean, Tom, I feel good, why?"

"You got out of hand singing karaoke, as usual."

"Oh great, was it that bad?"

"No, actually it was pretty good, you did Sonny and Cher's song 'I Got You Babe', you did Cher's part really well, I thought. And the bar did empty a bit. At least we were able to get good seats near the TVs to watch the hockey games. You have a knack for clearing the room, I must say."

Todd, being Todd and having an overwhelming desire to know all the gossip and latest rumors swirling around the bar, had to know what happened when Joe left the bar the previous night with this latest femme de fatale.

"Meant to ask you, Joe, you were looking a little cozy with that blonde over by the pool table last night, did you get lucky Sir Casanova?"

"Um, kinda, but I got robbed actually."

Todd perks up and raises his eyebrows. "What? How did that happen?"

Joe unabashedly recalls the steamy details of the failed encounter. "Well, we were getting cozy as you said, and one thing led to another, and we end up making out by my van outside when she suggests we take things a little more private. I figure maybe she has her own place; I am going in for the kill, but then she says it would be hot to do it in public. So, me being the romantic sort of guy I am, asks her if she would like to do it in the van right there in the parking lot. She says it sounded spicy, but no, a little more private than doing it right there and being seen by everybody at the bar. So, she suggests a park by a river."

Todd is riveted by Joe's story, or is this just some kind of crazy fantasy Joe concocted?

"So, then what, Joe, what happened?"

Joe continues, "so, we go to the Caloosahatchee River Park, and we are getting into it. I start to get undressed, and she sees that I am wearing those women's panties I wear."

Todd is very surprised hearing this detail and puts his hands up in a stop pattern. "Wait, hold up, women's panties?"

Joe smacks his forehead, just realizing he had relayed a little too much information, usually it was on a 'need to know basis' with others.

"Oops, did I say that out loud, damn."

Todd is instantly repulsed at that. "Why in God's name are you wearing women's panties? Are you a fag or bisexual or something?"

Joe backtracks and attempts to justify his actions. "No, it adds to the seduction, when I show them, it is a big turn on to most of them. Besides, I usually wear granny panties, not like a thong or something, that would be too weird."

Todd is unconvinced by his answer. "Seems kinda faggy to me."

Joe tries to divert Todd from the subject at hand and wants to get to the rest of his lurid story. "Yeah, I know, so anyway, we are getting down to business, I get in the back of the van, pull my pants down and turn around to see her pointing a gun at me and she tells me to hand over my wallet. I'm like, 'what the hell you doing, I am horny.' She said "I was not that good looking anyway and she had thought to roll me when we were playing tongue hockey at the bar, said my breath smelled and that's when she decided it wasn't worth the effort. She mentioned something about it being a favor she owed someone else or something."

Todd takes notice of that part and stays silent as Joe relays the rest of this ridiculous story. "

Joe is acting as if he is a conqueror of sorts. "Me being the stud I am, I try to get her to screw me anyway, then she can take my wallet. If that's what it takes to get her off, I figure it's worth a shot, might as well take the chance, right?"

Todd is in total amazement at Joe's revelation, his sense of being ignorant of potential danger. "So, you are sitting there in women's panties with a chick holding a gun on you and you still think you are going to get some, unbelievable!"

"Hey, you have to take it when you can. So, I think she mulled it over a minute and decides to give me a hand job out of pity, but she holds the gun on me still. Needless to say, I am not too turned on, but it was definitely different. So here she has my pecker in her hand and telling me to get harder and get it over with, or little Joey is going to be homeless. So, we are almost getting there when a police car pulls up and flashes its high beams at us. The officer gets out of his car, proceeds to mine and flashes his light in my face and asks us for ID, all that. That was a buzz kill, I was just about to..."

Todd raises his hands and tells Joe to not finish, he did not have to hear the sordid details.

"So, the officer finally leaves and tells us to wrap it up and depart, so I am still in the mood, when another car pulls up and honks it's horn and she says, 'Sorry Romeo, the party's over, my boyfriend's here to pick me up', and to hand over my keys and wallet to her, that it was fun while it lasted but all good things must come to an end.' I am incredulous and don't know what to say. Pisses me off, those were the only keys I had to the van, and it cost me $300 to replace them, not to mention having to get the locks replaced at my place."

"Joe, I can't believe what you get yourself into."

Joe agrees. "I just thought it might be a fun thing to try and look at what happened. Her boyfriend ruined it, I think."

17

One of the most common, engrained activities of Florida living is the open-air flea markets. You can find anything or anyone there.

Todd takes Joe to the local flea market to find used Ranger gear. He heard that the great Ranger goalie from the 70's, Eddie Giacomin, who hit bad times, recently sold some of his old gear and it was available there.

"What are we doing here at the Flea market, Todd?"

"I am just enjoying another Florida experience and thought you'd want to check it out." The sign in front of the flea market advertises that it is the world's largest flea market.

"It says it is the world's largest flea market, I wonder if that is true?"

"Sure, it is, Joe, till the next world's largest flea market is in Sarasota, and besides, where else can you still find lava lamps?" Joe picks up the lamp, looks at the bottom, and accidentally drops it, breaking it into little pieces.

"Joe, what are you doing now, someone is going to get hurt." They exit suddenly and unnoticed from the stand area. Todd is on the hunt for something specific. "I heard that Eddie Giacomin's used gear was available and thought I might see if I can afford it. Was there anything you would be interested in getting, Joe?"

"I came here for my special purchases, and I don't want to run into anyone I might know. Most of my friends are too classy to come to a joint like this."

"Oh, you mean like all our buddies down at The Goal Crease?"

"Yeah, something like that."

"And what special purchase, Joe?"

Joe starts to blush. "You know, those comfortable undergarments...."

"Oh, oh, the women's panties, you mean. I still think it's kinda faggy, dude."

Joe tries to quiet Todd as he looks around at the other customers. "Do you need to say that so loud?"

"Why, it's not like you know anyone here."

Todd meant to bring up the thing Joe mentioned the night before at the usual nightly get together at The Goal Crease when they became distracted.

Joe and Todd get in line to check out for his special purchase when he notices the cashier as someone he has hit on many times at The Goal Crease with no success.

"Oh, hi Mary, I didn't know you worked here. You never told me all those times we talked at The Goal Crease." Mary looks at what is in Joe's hands.

"Hi Joe, Todd, why are you buying these, do you have a new woman in your life that you never told me about? I thought you were single, at least that's what you tell me every time we chat at The Goal Crease."

"They're for my sick aunt back home in Buffalo. She can't get out, so I buy them for her and send them to her."

Mary is highly doubtful of Joe's flimsy excuse. "How old is your aunt, does she like bunnies, and these crotchless pairs don't make sense, is she still sexually active?"

"Ewww, ewww, ewww, no way, but what can I say, she likes to go al fresco."

Mary looks skeptically at another pair in the pile Joe is buying and holds them up to view. "These lacey ones seem a little racy for an old woman, are you really getting these for her, or do you have a stripper or something you're getting these for? I could see you doing that. You're such a player when I see you at The Goal Crease."

Joe throws up his hands in fake surrender. "you got me Mary…"

Todd jumps into the conversation immediately. "He buys them for himself, Mary. What are you embarrassed for Joe?"

Joe glares at his friend. "Thanks, old buddy, now I'll never have a chance to nail Mary," Joe says absent mindedly. But instead of getting turned off, Mary gets playful.

"Oh really, Joe, I am surprised. I think it's kind of hot, actually.

Joe perks up and senses his chance. He blurts out, "I have ones with kittens and duckies on them too, Mary."

"I did not think you were my type, Joe, but I am kind of turned on thinking about getting with you sometime to see you like that, how long have you been into this?"

Todd is astonished and cannot grasp what he is hearing. "You don't think it is gay, Mary?"

"No Todd, but for some reason it gets me a little hot."

Joe smiles at Todd. "See what I told you, Todd?"

"I still think it's a little queer, no thanks."

Mary wraps his purchase delicately, smoothing her hands over the bag, looking at Joe wistfully. "You know, Joe, I wonder how many of the guys are actually buying for themselves?"

Joe grabs his face pondering her question and looks around the place. "You mean you see other single guys come in and buy panties too, Mary? I wonder if I know any of them. Damn, I thought I was only one of a few that knew this trick."

"Yeah, you'd be surprised how many single guys buy panties here, like that Japanese guy behind you. I see him here often, and he even told me he wears them too, that it turns on the chicks. Maybe he is a long-lost twin of yours?"

Joe feels a twinge of jealousy and curiosity about the guy.

"Did you ever get turned on enough to want to be with him, Mary?"

"No, that would be wrong, he kind of creeps me out, besides I hear Japanese guys have small peckers, I need a real man. By the way, Joe, what are you packing in these panties?"

Joe winks flirtatiously at Mary, "let's just say big surprises come in small packages, why don't you see for yourself sometime, Mary?"

Todd can't take what he is hearing and witnessing and slaps his forehead. "Unbelievable, Joe, here we come in here to buy freaking women's panties for who I think is a mentally unbalanced guy and you might get laid out of the deal!" Todd storms off, heading to the food court to get a beer.

Joe thinks to himself, "I am curious about this other guy, maybe he belongs to a club or something that knows what I am doing.

He approaches the guy challengingly and spots women's undergarments in his hands. "Hey man, love the red panties, your woman is going love them."

The new guy hears Joe's comment. "Heah-ro." The man is speaking in a very heavy Japanese/ English accent.

"You really are playing up that Japanese accent, aren't you, dude?"

"No, I weally am fwom thar."

"Well, you definitely don't sound like you grew up here. So, are you really getting those for a 'special lady' at home?"

"Ah yes, she rikes to gibe me wound the wold with dese on."

Joe presses on, he's on a mission to find out what makes this guy tick. "Mary here seems to think you do not have a woman at home. So, what's the deal, it's cool if you are a pervert, I don't judge. My name is Joe, Joe from Buffalo and I don't mind telling you that I get these because I find it helps me get chicks. The women go crazy when they see me in them. Us he-men have to stick together; you know what I mean?"

The man seems embarrassed and unsure. "Ok, I found out about dat too."

"Cool, how did you discover that?"

The tone of the discussion changes slightly. "Whuy, are you ah gay or somefin, cuz I no putta my pecka in otha men."

Joe remains unfazed. "No, I am as he man as any other guy around, I was just wondering if you belong to a group or something, maybe we could trade techniques?"

The guy seems unswayed by Joe's line of questioning. "No, eastewn caltur encouwajs dibersity and diffewences."

Joe is perplexed but determined to get to the secret of this guy. "Huh, I always thought they are very rigid and against change?"

"No, ah we ar pwogwessive nowuh days"

"So, ok, do you get prime snatch wearing these?"

"I ah lika my snach ah young, yes, I get pwenty poosy."

"You never told me your name, friend."

"It is ah Tung Hang Lo."

Joe laughs hysterically thinking this guy is full of shit. He had never heard of such a name. "Tongue hang low, for real, you're not making that name up, don't bullshit a bullshitter, man."

"Ah, wella my name at biwth was Twuman Capot-a Wang."

"Why that name, that isn't Japanese sounding."

"My mom was a Twuman Capot-a fan."

Joe notices the unusual girth and length of his tongue as he is talking. "I can see why you changed it, but why that name? Oh, that is an unorthodox tongue span there. The women must love you."

"Ah yes, ah the womens lobe to get a Tung Hang Lo tweatment, is ah very speshal."

"I like your style, Tung, you should hang out with me and the guys at a place called The Goal Crease, just don't steal all the women there, I still have a few

I have my eye on, besides, new season begins soon and that means fresh meat. We watch hockey, do you follow hockey? They don't have sushi there at The Goal Crease, I'm afraid."

"Ah, yes ah I do."

"Do you have a favorite team?" "Ah, the Buffawo Sabwes."

"No way! I am from there, why do you like them?"

"We had a famos pwayer namead Tawo Tjusimoto who pwayed fow ah da Buffaro Sabwes."

"Dude, he was a made-up player that the then general manager Punch Imlach drafted as a joke."

"Ah, he big stawr in Japan, we ah even get repways of his goals. He ah even was ah wookie of the yeaw."

Joe shakes his head emphatically. "I am telling you dude, there was no such player."

Tung is unconvinced that this player was indeed real. "I ah can ah show you his famous pways on my ah cell phone, ah hewe."

Just then, Todd returns with two beers in his hand and a helmet with a flashing light and a beer strapped on the top with a straw that extends to his mouth. "Todd, do you see this supposed replay of a goal that the fake, made up player supposedly scored? Can you believe how fake it looks?" Joe shows Todd the grainy, fake hockey goal replay that is playing in loop form.

"It looks like a scene from that Godzilla episode where he wrecks that whole arena, remember that episode, Joe, and look, isn't that Godzilla in the background of this replay?"

Tung is convinced the video is real indeed. "Ah no, Tawo is weal pwaya and big staw in Japan."

"Did you ever meet him Tung?"

"Ah, no ah he wives in secwet spot where ah famous movie staws and famous empewers ah live."

Joe has heard enough. "Ok, Tung, don't get your panties in a bunch, oh, unless you're wearing some now, of course. Well, so if you want to hang out at the Goal Crease sometime, head up there. I like your style. Maybe you can give me some tips how to meet up with women." He turns to say goodbye to Mary. "See you at The Goal Crease, Mary."

Mary waves to Joe, Todd and Tung and is blushing now when she suddenly says, "Wear those bunny panties after I get off work, Joe, who knows, you might be fucking like them later."

18

Seeing famous and not so famous people around makes some people do things they'd normally not do. Joe and Todd were at their favorite place, you guessed it, The Goal Crease, one early evening. Todd was putzing around with his phone, Joe sitting there bored, staring aimlessly at the TV, when Todd looked up suddenly and points out a customer sitting at the bar, not far from where they were sitting. Todd punches stuff into his phone and pulls up a picture and shows it to Joe.

"Hey Joe, don't look too obvious but I think that's the ex-NHL player Kris Draper over there, remember him?" Todd discreetly raises his phone in the guy's direction and snaps a picture of the unsuspecting quasi-celebrity.

"Yeah, kind of, hell of a player if I remember but what would he be doing here in middle of winter, isn't he retired?"

Todd remembers useless stats on almost any hockey topic, and he recites immediately this hockey players stats as a school kid would recite a famous speech by Martin Luther King. "Drafted 3rd round by the Winnipeg Jets, played 1157 games, 161 goals, 203 assists, won the cup 4 times with the Red Wings, Frank Selke Award winner, pretty solid career."

Joe is unimpressed by the guy's stats or whatever, but it is kind of cool to talk to a real-life player, he thinks. "Eh, pretty average stats, but he played with some great players during his career. I gotta talk to him and let him know we're on to him."

"Joe, I don't think he came here to be bugged by a drunk, obnoxious Sabres fan."

"Hey, I'm not that drunk, and I wouldn't say I was a fan, he played for the Red Wings, not my team." Joe staggers over in a bold way and tries to get the attention of this stranger who is sitting quietly and does not seem to want any unnecessary attention.

Joe makes a poking gesture at him. "Hi, buddy, my friend over there, see him in the Rangers jersey, he told me you looked like a player from the Red Wings, and I have to say the picture he showed me looks exactly like you."

"Ha ha, buddy, no, it's not me, go back and have a few more dollar drafts."

The guy pulls back and faces another direction pretending to talk to a nonexistent person, but Joe is now determined to confront this guy and get the scoop on him and why he is here at The Goal Crease. "Are you sure it's not you, you look exactly like the picture, look here." Joe fumbles with his phone, he accidentally displays a nude photo on his cell, he abruptly deletes it and shows the picture from Todd's text.

The guy amusedly looks at Joe's proof and laughs. "Well, ok, I see the resemblance, but I swear it's not me, I don't even know what the Red Wings or whatever is."

The guy is obviously playing with Joe now, but Joe is determined to get him to admit he is who Todd says he is. "Are you sure, buddy, ok, if you don't know what the Red Wings are or whatever, who is the best hockey player you ever saw?"

The guy without hesitation blurts back "That would be easy, Bobby Orr, though Paul Coffey was a close second."

Joe's jaw drops and he points excitedly at the guy on his bar stool who is in a taunting reflex that Joe does not notice, he is in total disbelief. "You are telling me you're not a hockey player and yet you know who Bobby Orr and Paul Coffey is, here in Southwest Florida?"

"What can I say, I am well-traveled."

"How many Cup teams did you play on?" Joe now wants to play 21 questions with this seemingly uninterested chap.

The man now makes a serious face, and his eyes are twitching. "Buddy, I am telling you I am not who you say you think I am, but I think, four, winners that is, but that is if I am who you say I am, ha ha"

"So, ok, you played with my boy Dominik Hasek when he won the cup in 2002, would you say he was the best goaltender you ever saw?"

In the blink of an eye, he says, "He was great, but he was no Chris Osgood."

"See, I told you that you are Kris Draper."

"I have to go, nice meeting you." Just then, the man gets up and put his hands up in surrender mode, does not even pay his tab and leaves the bar.

"Way to go, Joe, scaring off a cool hockey player like that, we could have listened to some cool stories."

"What, Hasek was way better than Osgood, no big deal."

19

Joe tries to sneak in unnoticed by David who is in the garage closely observing his latest potato chip. He had heard it was a rare one with burn marks in it to make it appear to look exactly like Elvis Presley, sideburns, and all. Joe trips into the darkened living room and David comes into the place.

"What happened out there, Joe, why were you pulled over down at the end of our block?"

"I supposedly ran a stop sign and got pulled over. By the way, thanks for coming down the block and drawing more attention to myself, that is always welcomed, the flashing lights for half an hour on this block probably freaked out half the residents as it was."

"Anytime, Joe, I am the unofficial Crime Watch leader on the block and have to make sure everything is copacetic, and besides, seeing that I am the only white guy, I would never be accused of breaking into anyone else's house on our block."

"Yeah, I bet those are interesting block meetings."

"You were out there a long time, what did they get you for again?"

Joe raises his eyebrows and stares daggerlike at David. "At first, like I said, he pulled me over and told me I blew a stop sign, but then he ran my license and told me my license was suspended back home, I was genuinely surprised."

"And you did not get arrested, Joe, I am surprised."

"Gee, you say it like you are disappointed I was not taken in."

"Well, truth be told, I like my alone time. One needs a lot of time to devote to their potato chip collection."

"I am rarely ever here; you are alone here a lot. But, yeah, he took my license and then I returned to my van and drove back here, he must have thought I was a nut to do that. Besides, I am deliberately trying to stay under the radar, why would I go through a stop sign and draw attention?"

David scratches his chin. "Yeah, Joe, I can see you in front of the judge saying you did not want to 'draw attention to yourself'." He emphasizes the point by using air quote sign up in the air. "I feel that I was wrongly pulled over, besides, I was hurrying home because I was tired judge, which would go over well. "You are lucky they did not do a breathalyzer on you, I bet you were over the limit."

"This is unbelievable, I never had any run ins with the police ever my whole life, and since I have been down here, I have been pulled over more times than I ever was back home in all the years I lived there."

"Well, I'm sure you having NY plates has nothing to do with it."

"Yeah, it's pretty racist, you ask me, David."

"Sure, Joe, whatever you say, but it looked like a white cop that pulled you over. If it were Garcia, you would have been arrested, believe me."

Joe is fuming. "Exactly, smells of racism to me."

"Well, I told you that you've been pushing your luck driving around with those plates on, it's been, what, over a year now that you've been here, and driving around in that minivan makes the neighbors nervous. They think you are some kind of pervert or something driving around in it."

"This thing, why, it's my love van, chicks like it."

"If chicks like it, like you say they do, when was the last time you had a normal date not involving one of those floozies from The Goal Crease that you meet?"

20

Joe and Todd are at the Goal Crease, and two women walk in, one is quite heftier than the other. Joe has not had much luck lately and Todd is in his usual slump. Blame it on his too high standards. Todd has never been married, not even close to it. He has had a couple long term relationships, but the women were only interested in what he could do for them, not vice versa. In other words, what could Todd buy and give them? But Todd was not a shallow guy and wanted more than just a trophy on his arm, although truth be told, about now, even a booby prize seemed better than nothing. These two hit it off as friends and neither ever collided in matters of women nor even competed for the attention of any particular one. Joe spots the two women walking in gingerly, looking as though they are not sure whether to be at this hole in the wall or not.

"You take the skinny chick, Todd, I'll take the fat one."

"You are such a pig, Joe, why don't you ever give it a rest, man?"

"It's my mission to introduce as many chicks to Joey Casanova as humanly possible, my man. You have to get it while you can."

"Not for me, Joe, my days of skirt chasing are over. I think that chick I met at the hockey game the other night event is the one I am looking for, the trouble is she reminds me of the 46 Rangers, 22 wins, 32 losses, 6 Ties, 5th place finish that year."

Todd always believed his soul mate would be sitting in the 300 section seats at a minor league hockey game. "I suppose, yeah, I can see what you mean, Todd."

"How about you, Joe, how are things going with that chick, Marissa?"

"Oh, her, I don't know, alright, I guess. I have not seen her in a few weeks, and I am trying my darndest to be celibate for her. I don't know, there is just something different about her that draws me to her, not only sexually, although there is that of course." Joe lowers his voice and stares away from Todd. "But I did have another encounter the other night, not too memorable though it was the best BJ I ever got, swear to God. Chick off Craig's list, and she did not look anything at all like her picture."

"When are you going to learn, Joe, was she hot at least, do you have a picture of her I can see?"

"Depends on your definition of hot. Would a 220 pound, 60-year-old, 5-foot woman with a hump on her back qualify as hot?"

"What are you telling me, Joe, are you that hard up for pussy, dude?"

"Well, I was horny and needed to get off other than the usual way, lately, these days, you know what I'm saying?"

"Do you have a picture; I can't imagine how low you will go to get some."

"Yeah, ok, actually I do, here..." Joe is very hesitant but shows her picture to Todd and he gags holding his throat.

"Holy shit, Joe, how did you even get it up, some guys look better than her, not that I am gay or anything, but that is by far, the ugliest chick I think I ever saw, and you got with her?"

"Yeah, well, actually, she only gave me a blow job, and to be honest, it was the best one I ever had, swear to God, she even had a little surprise for me."

Todd stares at Joe in complete denial and shakes his head. "She didn't have a dick or anything, did she, a chick with a dick?"

"No, no, nothing like that, but get this, at first, I tried to leave when I saw what she looked like. We were in her bedroom, when she pushed me down on the bed, and popped her teeth out and said to lay back and close my eyes, I said, 'whoa, what are you doing?' I tried to push her off and she took charge, shoved me back down and forcibly unzipped my pants. She said, 'relax, her dead husband always told her she gave the best head', and I must admit, I could feel why."

"Joe, how could you even get hard, much less, get off?"

"Well, I laid back and closed my eyes and pretended she was a hot chick, and the fact is, the sensation of her sucking was as if a Hoover vacuum hose was wrapped around my member, it was incredible, Todd."

"How would you know how that feels, Joe?"

"That's a story for another time, buddy. But I have to tell you that was quite memorable, though when I opened my eyes and really saw what was happening and saw the way she was looking at me, I had to get out of there, pronto, or I felt like I was going to end up like that Hannibal Lector in the Silence of the Lamb movie, that would not have been pretty."

"Only you, Joe, only you."

21

Todd dials Joe's cell phone impatiently and waits for Joe to answer. Joe finally picks it up after 6 rings. "Joe, are you there, are you ok?"

"Yeah Todd, sure, why, you seem frantic, what's up, I'm just getting my nails done for my date later."

"Where are you now, Joe? I just saw a news report on TV about a late model silver minivan with wood grain panel plowing into the Taco Stand at the beach. The minivan drove down the bridge way too fast, missed the curve at the bottom, swerved uncontrollably and flipped upside down and hit the stand. It was a silver minivan and looked exactly like yours, I have driven with you, Joe and it seems like something you'd do."

"Gee, Todd thanks for the concern and doubt for your old buddy."

"Well, I could see you doing that, maybe got distracted by a hottie or something and lost control, just saying."

"Well, I don't blame you for coming to that conclusion, I have been having a bad string of luck lately regarding my driving performance, my brakes did go out again the other day." Joe gets a niggling feeling that this was no coincidence, but the van is pretty old and probably has not been worked on in at least a decade.

Todd tries to turn to a more serious issue. "Your accident made me realize how we are alone, and would not have an emergency contact if we had to go to a hospital or something, you know?"

Now Joe is starting to wonder about Todd's state of mind as he hears Todd carry on about this news story. "Whoa, whoa, whoa, Todd, not my accident, I was not the one that plowed into that taco stand!"

Todd continues as if he did not hear Joe deny his involvement in the accident, also thinking about the comment Joe made recently about the woman repaying a favor when she robbed Joe at that park. "If I were in an accident or injured, I know I wouldn't have anyone, have you thought about what you are going to do if something happened to you, Joe?"

Joe picks up on Todd's use of present tense but lets it slide. However, it does hit a bit of a nerve. Joe is down here on false pretenses, kind of, and he did not have the foresight to have contingency plans should something go afoul while he was here partying in Florida.

"By the way, Joe, you never really told me why you moved here in the first place, not that I am trying to get into your business or anything."

Time to deflect such inquiries, Joe thinks. "Just to have some laughs, meet a few chicks, have some fun Florida style, you, Todd?"

"Not going to sugar coat it or lie, to meet a rich chick that will take care of me, let me do what I want to do pretty much. I would prefer if she was hot and younger and loaded, I must maintain my high standards."

Joe does not want to burst Todd's bubble or let him down by pointing out the obvious. Even his friend Todd has fallen for the shallow, material world of physical looks and financial prowess as the reason to be with someone. "How's that going for you to this point, friend?"

Todd remains undeterred in his quest. "She is out there, Joe, trust me."

22

Sometimes you can go out looking for trouble but other times, trouble has a knack for finding you. Sometimes, the innocent and naïve cannot get out of their own way.

Rick hears his phone ringing, wondering who could be calling him at this time of day, when he usually spends his time taking care of his plants and bird sanctuary. 'This better be good', he thinks, as he answers his cell phone.

"Hey Rick, can you pick me up at county and post bail, I got into a little trouble."

"Sure, Joe' what's wrong?"

"I'll tell you when you pick me up."

Rick takes his time to kind of let Joe know that he's tired of bailing Joe out of everything. He cannot even understand his friendship with the guy. Joe constantly calls him when he needs this or that or can Rick bail him out of trouble like now. For some reason though, something about Joe and all his dilemmas makes Rick not only feel sorry for him but makes him empathize with him. Besides, Joe's problems and troubles pale in comparison with his own.

Rick pulls up in his very noticeable gargantuan pickup truck. The other prisoners hope it is them that he pulls into the lot to pick up. Then they see a short, older, balding guy waddling over, pull himself up into the front seat and propel himself into the truck. Joe's head disappears behind the tinted glass. Joe covers his face anyway, as if he is being stalked or hunted as a celebrity would be.

"So, ok, what did you do now, Joe? I knew I'd need that landline phone number to save your ass sometime. Was it drunk driving? I told you that your ways would catch up to you eventually."

Joe asks Rick to pick it up and get away from the holding center. "No, nothing like that, just a misunderstanding, kind of embarrassing actually."

"Well, I had to pony up a grand, so it had to be somewhat serious. What's it say on that piece of paper?"

Joe is waving the piece of crumpled up paper. "You mean this, it says violation of code 800.04."

"What does that mean, code what, what was it for?"

Joe is trying to act ignorant and evasive. "I don't know something about lewd and lascivious behavior, blah blah, blah."

"What do you mean lewd and lascivious behavior, uh oh, what did you do, Joe?"

"Well, you know how I got those high-powered binoculars because I've really been into bird watching lately?"

Rick feels as though he is being set up for a punch line. "Uh oh, so you were looking at young girls again, weren't you?"

"No, well, sort of, no, not really, not intentionally although tempting. No, I was at Hickey's Creek Park over on the Caloosahatchee. I came across a rare Painted Bunting, very rarely is it seen in these parts, so I was tracking it, maybe even get pictures of it to prove I saw it."

Rick is waiting for the shoe to drop. "Uh oh, Joe."

"How was I to know two 13-year-old girls would be skinny dipping in the river? They freaked out and called me an old pervert."

I wouldn't say you're that old, Joe."

"So anyway, the one jumped out of the water and grabbed her phone to call the police."

"Did you at least get a good look?"

"No, I screamed louder than them, even, turned to run the hell out of there only to run into a tree and a coconut fell out of it and hit me on the head. Next thing I know I'm being hauled away and brought to this place".

Rick turns to Joe in all seriousness. "Sounds like it was an accident, an innocent guy walking through the woods with military issued binoculars, what's the big deal?"

"It wasn't that Rick, I took pictures of the painted bunting, I did not have my glasses on and could not see clearly.

How was I to know nude underage girls were in the pictures? What really sucks is that the cops deleted the pictures, so now no one will believe I saw the painted bunting."

Rick tries to cheer his buddy up. "Too bad, Joe, there are those out there that would pay good money for those pictures, I bet."

23

Down here in South Florida, you either meet the sharpest shrewdest people you'll ever meet, or they are as dumb as rocks. Joe likes to think he is somewhere in between.

Although Joe had skipped out of town in Buffalo easily and was careful not to leave many clues about his whereabouts, it was not that difficult to find where he ended up. Even when some are trying to deliberately hide, they still leave obvious signs of their existence. Joe thought he had been cautious enough to change his usual stuff, including his ID, vehicle, address, the place where he chose to relocate, but even attention to details can be discovered if one looks hard enough. Even federal witness protection programs carefully set up to protect some have been known to fail. The group, or syndicate, as they liked to be known as, had far-reaching abilities in locating those that wanted to be gone and they were in the business of doing just that, making some be gone, even when they did not want to be gone. They had a limited budget, though, so finding the right "unwanted person's location services" was a little tricky. Through connections of connections, they discovered a rather low budget hitman that happened to be in between jobs but came highly recommended by Frank "The Goose" Siragusa who had a cousin, Jeremiah, who would freelance occasionally, especially if the jobs were in warm exotic locales. It did not take long to locate their mark, and they scheduled Jeremiah for a quick burn and turn job on an unsuspecting, gullible guy who was maybe the key to putting away a bad man back in Buffalo for a long time. The syndicate had gotten a lead that Joe was there when they intercepted decoded information about his whereabouts when an attempt was made at a park near Fort Myers. It was an insignificant report and would normally be ignored by those that check such inane police reports online but the vehicle identified was unusual and matched information the syndicate received regarding a late model silver minivan with woodgrain paneling was seen leaving Buffalo about the time a certain naïve, middle aged, balding, though good-looking guy was last seen around town. The syndicate had no connection to the attempted hit and/ or robbery attempt that occurred.

Jeremiah created an identity as a travelling pharma-ceutical sales rep and 'moved' to the town where this mark sat like a pigeon. Jeremiah arrived in town between Thanksgiving and Christmas, the perfect time to be away from up north, and although it was supposed to be easy to find this character, Joe, he had little luck at first. Jeremiah, and even the syndicate could not easily monitor the movements of a wandering nomad such as Joe. Jeremiah tried every possible way to locate this guy, this was such a small town, where could this guy be? Jeremiah's idea to find this guy was unusual, he would drive down main roads from 11-3 every day and his success rate at finding the wanted was surprisingly meager.

A few days before Christmas, the syndicate was about to pull the plug on their search, and Jeremiah was in the process of getting out of town, when he aimlessly wandered into a small dumpy unnoticeable joint called The Goal Crease for a drink. He asked the bartender to throw on the Philadelphia Flyers game and was not paying any attention, when a short, older, balding guy in floral patterned swim trunks and a striped shirt approaches and startles him.

"You gotta love the holidays, brings out the best in some of us. Looks like I am not the only loser in town that has no one to spend Xmas with, the Flyers, huh? You must be from Philly?"

"No, the DC area actually."

"You people and not following your hometown teams, what is up with that, what's wrong with the Caps? I am Joe, Joe from Buffalo, you?"

Jeremiah shakes his head in denial, there is NO WAY on earth this could have happened. He pulls his phone out to check the picture the syndicate sent him. Sure enough, this is this guy, but Jeremiah cannot tip his hand and needs to play it cool, work his way into it and finish the job. "My name is Jeremiah. I can't stand them or any sports team, period, there. They are boring and never won anything."

Joe is engaged to speak with a hockey fan like himself. "Boring, what about Ovechkin?"

"He is a crybaby, and Russian. I don't trust Russians, they even cheat when they are drinking vodka." Jeremiah keeps up the ruse and remembers he is supposed to be a pharmaceutical sales rep.

"You live here or just passing through?"

"Live here in this God forsaken place, now."

What do you do?"

Jeremiah looks around to make sure no one is watching him and pulls large sunglasses over his eyes."Um, sales rep."

"Cool, I used to be a sales rep, what do you sell?"

Jeremiah wanted to appear standoffish and uninterested, yet he had to draw Joe in a bit more to make sure he was the one that Jeremiah was sent to dispatch. "Pharmaceutical drugs."

"Cool, always a need for that, especially down here, where do you work?"

"Main office is in Miami, but I am the west coast sales rep for them."

"The west coast, huh, of here, Florida, or the whole country?"

"My territory goes from here down to Key West, where we get our shipments." 'Ok, easy Jeremiah', he thinks to himself, don't overplay it.

"I never knew Key West was such a big port for commerce."

"Oh, a lot of tonnage of product comes through. There are enough clients here in this region that they hired a regional rep to handle the influx of business, especially the seasonal business."

Joe is genuinely interested in this tale being spun. "It seems that there are that many people that need these drugs that they are expanding, I imagine?" Joe attempts to demonstrate some sort of in-depth knowledge of the area. "There are a lot of retirees here, and, oh, Mexicans."

Jeremiah is starting to wonder what direction this conversation is taking now. "Yeah, actually some of them are our competition."

"Whoa wait, how are they your competition?"

Jeremiah catches himself and tries to make things sound legitimate. "They came out with a generic, low-priced product, er, drug that is killing our market share, so we had to expand to compete."

Jeremiah thinks he sounds believable enough even though in real life he was an unsuccessful health club trainer that kept losing clients so much, that the club demoted him to pool cleaner after the senior citizens' water aerobics class every morning. Talk about a "crappy" job.

"Sounds interesting." "

Yeah, we are killing them, I mean, it, now."

Joe is pulled in completely by this tale spun by Jeremiah. "I never heard of a Mexican Pharmaceutical company, what are they, like Pfizer or something?"

"No, more like a cartel." 'A cartel, stupid, stupid, stupid, stupid, stupid, stupid', thinks Jeremiah, this guy will definitely know this is all fake.

Luckily, Joe never heard of a cartel and even goes so far as to offer his assistance. "Well, if you ever need help or hiring more guys, let me know."

Jeremiah sizes up Joe. "We have size requirements; I don't think you'd measure up."

Joe is ready to depart and, as an afterthought, asks Jeremiah what he was doing the next day. "So, what are you doing for Xmas, Jeremy? I am meeting my buddy Rick down at the beach, thought it would be cool to spend Xmas at the beach. Wanna go?"

Jeremiah is jolted. This is like letting the fox into the chicken coop, it can't be this easy, can it? "It's Jeremiah, sure, I'm not doing anything, the hit, or it, can wait till Monday".

24

It was going to be his first Christmas in Florida away from everyone, the snow, and the cold, so Joe pushed his new friends Todd and Rick to do something beachy, go figure? They agreed it would be fun to do a pub crawl, of sorts, along the beach. Surprisingly, the nightlife there was more active than Joe thought it would be. No one at the beach got the memo that Florida was supposed to be an early turn in kind of place. So, Rick, Todd and Joe start Happy hour at their favorite place, of course, the place with the 99 cent drafts and $5 appetizers, the perfect combination, cheap and cheap. They were into their third, or fourth when Joe mentioned to Todd that he just met another cool dude from DC.

"Hey Todd, I met a guy called Jeremy or something from DC, but get this, he follows Philly teams, not even Washington ones, what's with you guys following sports teams from other cities?"

"It's a level of sophistication you'll never understand, Joe."

"So where else are we gonna go, Todd, it's kind of lame here."

Rick pipes in, "Yeah, in other words, Happy Hour prices are over, we get it Joe, where did you park again, down the beach about a mile and you want us to end up closer to your car, I bet?"

Joe grins devilishly. "Well, if we end up that way, I won't mind, where next?"

There was a place across the street dividing the beach, into a little joint that, sure enough, had live music and lots of gorgeous, hopefully desperate, and horny vacationers looking for a little fun. Joe noticed he was loosening up now that he was in town for just under a year, he still lives way out in Bumfucksville and his social activities are limited to occasional visits to the local gin joints there and hanging out with Todd and Rick at The Goal Crease, enjoying $ Bud drafts and the occasional $5 burger night. Life was good and it seemed like he was comfortable and safe here in Fort Myers. Oh sure, living in that desolate, isolated house 20 miles from everything was kind of boring but he was still able to get to the beach often, see his buddies and basically enjoy carefree Florida living as it was meant to be. The third stop of their journey involved being transported. Rick decided at the last minute while they were at the place with the live music that he needed fresh air, so he decided to walk down the beach. Next thing Joe knows, he got a call on his phone.

"Joe, you and Todd have to head over to where I am, it's a cool joint down the beach, they are giving away free pizza and stuff." Free has an effect on Joe, so he told Rick they'd be right there. Joe tells Todd where Rick says he was and he tells him that it is about two miles away and that he isn't walking there, free pizza and all.

"I suppose I can drive, Joe but I will be giving up my prime spot over at The Beached Whale. I was planning to keep the car there till the end of the night." So, Todd and Joe jump into the car to meet up with Rick. The place is also having a Christmas karaoke night.

Joe lights up when he sees that karaoke is happening at the little place.

"Oh wow, Rick, I love doing karaoke, especially Christmas songs, I can't wait to sing."

It is Joe's turn, and he selects 'Silent Night'. As Joe is singing, people start booing and staring incredulously at him, some put their hands over their ears, others pointing their phones at Joe, still others getting up and walking out the door, but Joe doesn't care. He is having so much fun and doesn't want the night to end. After he finishes, he walks up to Todd and Rick, who are laughing hysterically.

"What, haven't you heard that version of Silent Night before?"

"Joe, I've never in my life heard that version, you really got a reaction."

"Cool, Todd, thanks, I can't wait to do another song". Joe eagerly walks up to the DJ to pick his next song, and she tells him they are finished, that the whole playlist has been used already. Joe's mood changes immediately and he is incensed and wants to do another song, but the DJ steadfastly refuses to let Joe sing again. Joe is steamed and decides he will never again grace this establishment and give them his paltry Budweiser draft business in the future.

25

Joe was moving slightly slowly this morning from his previous night's debauchery and was hung over. It's Christmas morning and he is not feeling too jolly. He stumbles into the kitchen and starts to make some coffee. He hears David whistling an upbeat tune and wonders what's up with that?

"You got in late, you party rocker."

Joe really did not want to explain his previous night's raucous behavior, and he wanted to give the impression that he was with a chick the night before. He did not want to let David think he did not really want to hang out with him just because it was the holidays. "Yeah, I had a date with a little cutie."

"Oh, what was his name, ha ha?"

"Ha, funny. Actually, I got tossed from the Lighthouse again." A little misrepresentation or exaggeration never hurt, thought Joe.

Even though Joe had not lived there that long, David had heard this all before. "Joe, did you try to hump the cigarette machine in the corner again, what happened now?"

"Long story, but I couldn't help the bitch was not a fan of Kiki Dee."

"Kinky Who?"

"Gal that did a duet with Elton John back in the 70's."

"Ah, and you sang the chick's part, huh, you sure you aren't taking the high, hard one down the poopchute?"

Joe points at David determinedly and puffs his chest out. "How many times do I have to tell you, David, I am a bonafide man's man."

David is unconvinced. "I don't know, just the women's panties, singing female parts to songs, just seems different to me, is all."

"Well, I admit, I have a sensitive side to me, but I am into chicks, trust me dude."

"Ok, ok, don't get your panties into a bunch again." David looks at him and shrugs. "So, what's going on today, Joe?"

"The usual, nightly stop at the Goal Crease." Joe saw David's reaction and did not really care to invite David out; it seemed like he was looking to be invited out but Joe had previous plans with the guys and did not feel like having to lug David around and tries to distract him from that. "Huh, what, I like the ambience, that, and the dollar drafts. But I have been meaning to check out that little place over on 41."

"You gotta love those small places, Joe."

"That's what she said, David, that's what she said."

26

The guys had a somewhat tumultuous start to their burgeoning friendships and Joe seemed to forget that he was still being hunted down by some unknown group, maybe even close to being arrested. He decided he was gonna live for the moment, throw all caution to the wind. Things had gone much better than he could have ever imagined when he arrived here and despite a few obstacles, some misunderstandings and excuseable dalliances with the law, he was in a good place and did not want to blow it. He decided to make a better effort to change some things, but some things are easier said than done.

27

There is no way better way to spend Christmas day than at the beach, the surf, the sand, the sun and warmth makes you feel so alive. Of course, there can also be challenges in just such a setting.

It is early in the morning; Joe is a little slow from the antics from the night before. He luckily ditched David and was set to 'let the day go where it goes'. The last time Joe saw Rick was at that place, he forgot where, but it was pretty late. Joe thought he saw Rick hooking up with someone but lost track when he went on his own expedition for cheap burgers after midnight.

"Merry Christmas, Rick, where's that chick you hooked up with last night, I thought she was heading down with you?"

"Her name is Angelina, eh, she's a whacko."

"Why do you say that?"

"Well, we were out last night having a few, well, ok, maybe more than a few as you know, and we start to head back to her place here on the beach, then she snaps just like that."

"What do you mean, why?"

"Well, we got asked to leave the bar after closing time, I did not want to do my usual and sleep it off in the truck on the beach, the cops don't like that so much here, I'm told. So, when she told me she had a place close by, I took my truck, and she went with me. I am driving along all well and fine, and she gets all worked up. She's telling me to slow down and stop swerving all over the road and to slow down, some people don't know how to have fun, you know? She got pissed and said she would never drive with me again, oh well."

"So, what did you do after, did you stay there anyway?"

"Yeah, but things did not go so well. I told her I was hanging out with you and then she went off about how much we drink, blah, blah, blah."

Joe shrugs nonchalantly, putting his hands out, palms up. "Well, we do always end up at a bar somewhere when we say we want to hit the beach, I don't have much of a tan, I think it's code for 'let's go get slammed at happy hour at the beach."

Just then, Joe looks up and sees the woman he remembers he thought Rick hooked up with the previous night. It was Angelina rambling along down by the water away from Rick and Joe, but close enough to be seen by them.

Joe sees her waving a finger at them. "Was that just her that walked by giving you the finger, geesh?"

"Some people take things too seriously. Oh, here she comes again, I wonder what she wants?"

Angelina strolls by again and abruptly stops at the shore and turns back and heads over to the guys. "You fucking asshole, I thought we were going to spend the day together."

Rick stares at her and back at Joe and mutters, "I told you I made plans to hang out with Joe, you could come along."

Angelina is beside herself at this point, her plan was to snag a willing, available guy with money, move him into her place and pay the rent for her. The problem was, she was not a younger, gorgeous directionless starving college or ex college student but an older, used up hag that got her kicks singing karaoke nightly at The Lighthouse and other similar such pseudo tiki bars found along the shores here in Fort Myers.

Rick had his doubts when one of her friends the very night he first met her, asked Rick outright if he was Angelina's new squeeze? It was as if she was too quick to snag someone.

She showed signs of bipolarity. "I want you to get all your shit out of my place immediately and I am putting a restraining order on you, you asshole, and they won't be using peach fuzz handcuffs like you used on me last night. by the way, my ass is still sore, you jerk off."

"What, I thought you enjoyed it, you said you wanted it rough."

Angelina will hear none of it and raises her voice so loudly that others can hear her yelling, even over the sound of the waves crashing on the beach.

"If you ever come down here to the beach, I am going to have you arrested, this is my beach, not yours. I will have a restraining order put on your ass so fast you won't know what hit you." She points her fingers and pokes Rick roughly on his chest.

"Wow, Rick, why was she so steamed, I saw her poking you in the chest too."

"She is a complete nutjob, Joe, it was just a night, sheesh, what the hell?"

Another beachgoer gets up off his towel and walks up to Rick and Joe, who are staring at her as she walks off defiantly. "Hey, you alright buddy, I saw the way that woman was freaking out on you, I am a police officer from Cape Coral, and I deal with whackos like that a lot, are you ok?"

"Yeah, I am, just that I might need help getting my stuff later, but anyway, thanks".

Joe spots the guy Jeremy or whatever his name was, from The Goal Crease the other night. He felt bad for this younger guy, he did not seem to have anyone else he knew from the area, so Joe, being the friendly, caring type he was, had invited him to the beach. Little did Joe know, Jeremiah knew exactly who he was already and had accidentally enjoyed this supposed random meeting the other night, to set up Joe and eliminate him from possibly providing evidence to put away those nasty dudes from Buffalo that he had seen by accident. It was now Jeremiah's contract to squish this gnat and move on to his next job.

"Oh, look, it's that guy I mentioned to you, Jeremy, he said he was going to meet us down here."

This behemoth Jeremiah saunters up the beach, squinting and looking around suspiciously. Rick notices his approach and shady gestures, greeting this stranger wearily but not coming across skeptical. "Hi partner, name's Rick, I heard about you from my buddy Joe, it's Jeremy, right?"

Jeremiah looks at Joe in disdain, shakes his head and thinks to himself what an idiot this guy Joe is, and how Joe, to his own lack of awareness and knowledge, will enjoy his limited participation in life the next few days or so.

"It's Jeremiah, Joe must have told you who I was."

Rick notices his build and mannerisms but keeps his thoughts to himself.

"You are a big guy, Jeremiah, did you play football or something?"

"No, I ran and played lacrosse."

Rick knowingly makes an obvious insult. "You got to be kidding me, you look like a sumo wrestler, I can't believe you were nimble enough to be a lacrosse goalie."

Joe gets impatient with this seemingly meaningless excuse for politeness and discussion and has his mind on one thing, and one thing only. "Well, it's almost noon, where are we going for Happy Hour first?"

Rick picks up the desperate cue from Joe to have fun today, no matter his alarms go off about this new guy, Jeremiah.

"Let's head over wherever and let the day go where it goes, guys, let's just hope we don't run into the Queen of Fort Myers Beach".

Rick responds quickly, "You mean more like the Witch of Fort Myers Beach."

The guys leave their stuff at the beach and proceed to Joe's favorite watering holes. Rick can't believe how many places Joe seems to know even though he has only been here a short time, but they have drinks and sometimes even appetizers at some of the places, and time drifts away until Jeremiah notices it's getting late. Rick steers them to one last place he had heard about from the bitch, Angelina.

"This place looks pretty cool, Rick, what's it called again?"

"The Lantern or something, I think."

"No, it says Lighthouse or something. I don't see any light houses around here, do you, Jeremy?" Joe says, using Jeremiah's name incorrectly for about the fourth time today, already.

"No, Jackass, I don't see no lighthouses."

"It's Joe, why do you keep saying my name wrong, it's an easy name to remember, Joe from Buffalo, it rhymes."

That, in Jeremiah's mind cements that this character Joe is who he is after, how easy was this?

Joe gets distracted by a guy setting up cheap microphones and a speaker system that looks like it was a Radio Shack karaoke machine from the 80's. "Oh cool, they are doing karaoke, I have been known to do a great rendition of Elton John's 'Don't Go Breaking My heart', with Kiki Dee, remember that song, Rick?"

"No, Joe, but hopefully the whacko won't show up here. I am told she is a regular and has been known to be here pretty much every night."

Joe is surprised to hear his name called so quickly to do his song, he rushed over to a non-English speaking tourist wearing a man's thong bathing suit, flowered shirt and straw hat and asked him if he would do a duet with him. Little did he know Joe was singing the female part.

"Ok, guys, I am up next, found someone to do Elton's part."

Joe and his unsuspecting participant of karaoke break out into song when Rick notices that Joe seems to be doing the female's part of the song, although he did not know the actual song, he had heard it a few times. He starts to notice that the other patrons are getting listless and unhappy about this screeching coming from the stage area. It is a duplicate of events that occurred just the night before when they were pub crawling.

"Jer, why are people making catcalls and throwing cans at Joe, he doesn't sound that bad."

"See that old lady over there, she seems to be getting under his skin, what's Joe yelling back at her?"

Joe throws down the microphone and makes a boxer pose and rushes to get in the surprised lady's face, Joe spitting in her face.

Rick is trying to interpret this confusing scene of his usually happy-go-lucky friend now exaggeratedly yelling and pointing at the frightened, older, frail looking lady. Rick overhears Joe say to her, "go fuck herself and that he did her granddaughter last night." The woman says her granddaughter was only 13." Then Joe says loud enough for everyone to hear, "oh, that explains why she was calling me daddy last night."

Rick does not want to get involved in Joe's stupidity when he looks over and sees Jeremiah immersed in his own phone, not paying attention to the ruckus Joe is creating. "Hey Jeremiah, you're missing the action, why are you on your phone so much, it's Christmas."

"Pharmaceuticals is a 24/7 business, Rick."

Rick did not get that vibe from Jeremiah, that he was a pharmaceutical sales rep, much less a professional of any kind. He could not put his finger on it, so he let it go for now. He would get to the bottom of this Jeremiah character at some point, but for now he was watching Joe make a complete ass of himself.

Joe is incensed that this rude lady had interrupted his creation and continues insulting the poor woman, when her angry husband decides to get involved. Rick overhears Joe saying something about knocking him out of his argyle socks if he doesn't mind his own business. Rick ducks away and doesn't want the others to see that he has been with Joe, and he goes out to the parking lot to wait for Joe there.

The shift manager grabs Joe to settle him down. "Um, sir, we have to ask you to please leave."

Joe leaves the place dejectedly and does not see Rick or Jeremiah. He figures he will have to catch a cab back to his place, worse yet, maybe walk because he is broke.

Luckily, he spots Rick over in the lot where they started this God-awful day. Rick speaks from the dark, his face covered. "You sure know how to bring down the house, Joe".

"I didn't think I was that bad, was I Rick?"

"Joe, does a hobby horse have a hickory dick?"

Joe looks quizzically over at Rick. "What, I can't help she didn't like Kiki Dee."

28

As many do every year, they make resolutions to change something from the past, improve something or change old habits. It was just under a year that Joe had been here, he made a few friends, oh sure, he got into a little trouble here and there, but for the most part, things improved for him but he hoped to meet someone new to enjoy things with so he decided that would be his challenge for the upcoming year. But old habits sometimes die hard.

Joe and Todd are sitting at the Goal Crease for their usual Monday night burger special. Todd is fidgeting with a small device on the bar. Joe is not paying attention to what Todd is doing. A pretty lady swaggers by, Joe is fixated on her wiggling ass as she walks along the length of the bar.

Todd sees Joe's fixation and interrupts his too long gaze. "Hey Joe, I did not think listing four hours of sex from the other night on the Diet and Exercise program at work counts as cardiovascular activity, and first of all, I doubt you can last 4 hours much less 4 minutes. I've seen some exaggeration in the past, but this takes the cake."

Joe, answers in a hushed tone, so as not to let the others at the bar overhear him speak lightly. "Why not, Todd, the new girlfriend got me sweaty and made me breathe heavily afterwards. She's pretty acrobatic and gets the heart racing if you know what I mean. Acrobatics is included in the list. She is definitely flexible and got me into some challenging positions, my left ear is still a little sore."

Todd motions for Alex to get him another Bud dollar draft. "Wait a minute, did you call her your girlfriend? By the way, Joe, was that her that was up here at The Goal Crease the other night? She looks young enough to be your granddaughter, much less your daughter. She definitely did not look old enough to drink legally. You should stick with women your age. You are out of control, you know that, Joe. I never know who you are with these days; most of them, you could end up in jail for being with them."

"Eh, she told me she was old enough, why would she lie? Besides, she only calls me when she is bored and has nothing better to do, but it works for me. She gets what she wants, and I get what I want." Joe twitches nervously, his eyes blinking rapidly.

"I heard she tossed her cookies in the bathroom the other night Joe. Everybody keeps talking about it."

"Yeah, I'll never hear the end of that one, I'm afraid. Why don't they get a life and worry about themselves, Todd?"

"You seem to contribute to a lot of people's delinquencies, Joe, what was she drinking to make her do that?"

"I don't know, I lost track after the 5th Fireball shot, she must be a lightweight, I guess. Thing that sucks is every time I bring someone new here something goes wrong, I don't need no drama, this is my place, I don't need someone to mess it up."

Todd takes a bite from his juicy hamburger, a small drool coming out of the left side of his mouth. "True Joe, but I think the only reason you feel like that is because you are too cheap to find another place that offers dollar drafts and tolerate you at the same time. Maybe you need to find another place?"

29

In his effort to stick to his New Year's resolution, he decided that to meet someone would mean changing his usual pick-up lines and feeble attempts at hooking up at places like The Goal Crease and tiki bars. He decided he'd make an effort to go on a regular date with his new love interest, a very much younger woman that sparked his curiosity.

"Gee, Joe, I did not realize how many people despise you around town, we can't go anywhere without people yelling "get out of town, Joe from Buffalo'."

"I can't help it I leave a good impression everywhere I go, what can I say?"

"I don't know, Joe, that one lady said she never wants to see you again or she'd call the cops."

"Some people never forget their little grand-daughter is a slut, geesh."

Marissa shakes off Joe's inane comment and attempts to change the subject "I like your mismatched outfit of floral pattern shorts and striped shirt, was that as a memento of our first night we met?"

"Not really, it's kind of my usual wardrobe, but um, yeah, first night thing."

Marissa looks down at the obvious plastic flowers Joe brought as a romantic gesture on their date. "Thank you for the plastic flower bouquet, too, nice touch for our date."

"You're welcome, Marissa, I thought they'd last longer than real flowers, besides you'd be surprised what one finds at a funeral at the cemetery."

Marissa is seated at the booth of the restaurant and looks around." Where did you find out about this place, anyway, it has a unique ambience?"

"Yeah, it's called Chick Fil-A, and there was a groupon for it, so win, win. I hope you don't mind us going halfsies, you just have to pay your share. I get my meal free, but drinks are included, I don't want to be a cheapskate."

"So sweet of you, Joe, I never had anyone do such a nice thing, thanks." Joe is determined to try to be interested in her unlike his other conquests where he was usually only interested in one thing.

"So, Marissa, I want to know all about you, tell me everything."

"Not much to tell you, Joe, I am guessing we have a lot in common."

"Oh, how did you guess that Marissa, do you wear women's underwear too?"

"Joe, that's for me to know and you to find out".

Joe can barely contain himself in public. "MMMM, I like how this is going so far, Marissa."

"Now, now, calm down big guy, some mystery and intrigue make things more exciting, a little art of seduction, a 'dance' is more titillating, don't you think? I heard from Todd that you have a number of conquests, I am not that type of person, I want a total commitment, or I am gone."

Despite his sudden urges, he fights off his usual response in these situations and thinks about his pledge to change those habits. "No, Marissa, I want that, and you seem to be what I am looking for, I just can't put a finger on it, something about you, I don't know."

"Well, if you want all this, Joe, I just want you to be sure."

The old Joe comes out anyway. "Can't I just get a little sampling after, Marissa? I mean, come on, we are on an actual date, I even paid for your drink, Marissa."

"Is this where you bring all your dates, Joe, am I just another notch on your belt?"

"No, baby, I don't think of you like the others, I can tell you're different from all the others."

"More than you know, Joe. I am looking for my soulmate, someone I can be myself around, not have anyone judge me like the others."

"Who would judge you, Marissa, you are perfect in my eyes. Now, doesn't that earn me a little action yet?"

"Oh, Joe, you are such a player, aren't you? I don't believe you, yet you did bring me these sweet flowers and kind of pay for dinner."

"Little Joey just wants some, that's all, it's his fault, not me, saying this, I swear."

"Aw, now you're ruining it and making me not want to do anything with you till we tie the knot."

"Please, baby, please, I won't brag to my friends like the other times. I'll even wear my pink see through lace undies for you."

"As enticing as your delectable offer is, Joe, let's finish our sandwiches wrapped in foil and cool down, big boy. I don't want this to be a one-night thing and you move on to the next floozy. I am telling you I am different than all the others you've been with, trust me."

"I believe you, Marissa, I just can't put a finger on why I believe it, ok sure, my right hand late at night in my bed at David's, not that he hears anything."

"You are too cute, Joe, I could just eat you up."

"Be careful what you say, you just might have to do it, so where do we go from here Marissa? I met you that night out before Thanksgiving, we went all up and down the beach with Rick, Todd, and the gang. I did everything I could do to get you to not like me, yet you keep showing up, like that time I mentioned to you that Rick was down at the beach, and you went down there with your sister to mooch drinks off him. That's when I knew we were meant to be. But Rick still bugs me about the $129 I owe him for that, some guys never leave stuff alone, I guess."

"I don't know, Joe, it seems like you're the one always pursuing me."

"Ok, I guess we'll take it slow, you sure you don't want to go back to my van and play "Pop Goes the Weasel" with little Joey?"

30

Despite Joe's best intentions to want to stay loyal to only one chick, he had previously committed to attending a dating site's sponsored event at a local hotel that was decorated in cheesy Valentine's Day décor to give the appearance of newfound love and hope.

"Are we that desperate to hook up to go to a POF get together to meet chicks, Todd?"

"Not all of us are a pig like you and fuck anything that breathes, Joe, some of us have standards."

"Well, Todd, at least I get action once in a while, no matter how unconventional and vile it is at times, besides, I just haven't found the right one yet. Marissa shows promise but she won't give it up yet."

"No, thanks, Joe, I have seen some of your dates. I suppose you are going to unveil your secret weapon to some unknowing, desperate, raving alcoholic that won't know what hit her again?"

"Ah, Todd, I should only be so lucky, you are too picky, I think. I am not so shallow as to only judge someone on their looks like you do. I value other traits and characteristics.

"Yeah, Joe, I guess you set the bar so low, how can you miss, right?"

"Where were we going again, seems like we have been driving awhile?"

"It's out in Cape Coral, I figure no chicks out here will know either of us and we will have a good shot at meeting some unsuspecting victims."

"I heard Cape Coral chicks are easy, Todd, who knows, maybe you will actually meet one with a full set of teeth and no freckles or the old, widowed ones like the ones you seem to meet at The Goal Crease."

"Remind me why I keep taking you places with me Joe?"

"Because you have no other friends that understand your passion for the sport of hockey, particularly the Rangers. Nice touch with the matching Ranger socks and tie, no woman will be able to resist that. Besides you know I am a party of one and can pull in the crowds, even if they get a little violent at times." The two reach their destination, and head inside to the event.

"Ok, Joe, we are there, I think it would be better to break apart, survey the prospects and meet over at the bar and compare notes."

"Geesh, it's not like we have the same tastes in women, Todd, but ok, I'll play along for shits and giggles. I already got my eye on a cutie, anyway, Todd, see you later." Joe walks around dressed in his usual outfit of flowered swim trunks and striped shirt. He notices the others parting for him in every place, but he is oblivious about his outfit. "Hi, my name is Joe, Joe from Buffalo, how and who you doing?"

"Not doing you, that's for sure, creep, get lost." The woman pushes Joe away from her open handed.

"That was pleasant and humbling, Miss, you did not even give me a chance to impress you and tell you some of my deep, dark secrets that many chicks have fallen for, but your loss."

"Get away from me, Joe from Buffalo, or I am going to have my Roller Girls from the local Roller Derby team roll your ass."

Joe reacts, "Ha, oh I bet they are so tough, they are not as tough as hockey players. Where are these supposed friends now?"

"Standing right behind you, you midget."

Standing directly behind Joe are a couple beautiful yet well-toned and defined ladies. Joe is not intimidated, actually he is turned on. "Oh my, those are some very large, muscular, toned women, yum, I could handle a Roll on the Rink with them anytime."

One of her friends notices this creepy guy in a weird outfit standing too close to the other girl. "Gina, is this guy bothering you, do you need any help?"

"No, Lola, he was just leaving, weren't you, Joe from Buffalo?"

The other lady perks up at the mention of his name. "Did you say Joe from Buffalo, Gina? I saw his posters plastered down at the Beach; he is not allowed in most places. Something about horrible karaoke singing, I think."

Joe is now offended. "Hey, my karaoke is great, just because I do the women's songs, are you jealous or something, Lola, because you know you can't belt it out as good as I can? Joe becomes distracted by another cutie. "But wait, Gina, who is that hottie to the right of Lola, is she a stuck-up bitch like you are?"

Lola comes to the aid of her friend. "Who did you call bitch, you impotent, pathetic limp dicked loser?" She goes to grab Joe and remove him from the immediate area.

"Ouch, get your hands off my ears, Lola or I will slap you silly." Joe goes to slap Lola in the face when Lola dekes him out and lands an upper cross punch across the bridge of his nose.

The host and a group of onlookers approach Joe to protect the woman. "Sir, this is not the intended actions we expect our clients and guests of POF Meet and Greet night to act, we are going to have to ask you to leave."

"Fuck you, I don't want to be here anyway, you all are a bunch of losers that can't find no real guys, look at what you're missing out on." Joe flashes his silk black see through thong hidden under his pants.

Gina is unimpressed by his childish display. "Yeah, thank God, freak, buh bye."

Joe walks to the parking lot and is sulking. "Where did Todd go? If he doesn't get out here in 5 minutes, I am going to leave him here with that nasty ugly ass, gross plus sized Amazonian women, they aren't even that hot."

A good amount of time passes, and Joe is getting very impatient, but he is stuck in the parking lot and can't even sit in Todd's car.

Todd comes out smiling awhile after, not having noticed Joe's absence. "Geesh, Joe, now what happened, we were barely there 15 minutes or so."

"I can't help lesbians show up at these things, thanks for ruining my night, Todd."

"Well, Joe, I think I met someone even though we were only there a short time."

"Oh, Todd, who is she, where is she, what does she look like, let me take a gander?"

"Slow down, Casanova, I am not showing or telling you who she is, so you don't go ruining my last shot at happiness with someone I've been looking for my whole life."

"Oh, you mean, the possible future ex-wife, Todd? Where does she live, what does she do?"

"I am not sure, she was obscure and vague, but I got her number and even though she saw what an ass you are, she must like me."

"Did you give her your number like you always do, using famous Rangers players' numbers to decipher it?"

"Of course, yeah, Robbie Ftorek, Glen Sather, Rod Gilbert, Barry Beck, John Davidson, Adam Graves, Joe, why?"

"Oh brother."

31

Joe had not been around the past few days and David did not seem to care or mind. Joe would do that occasionally. As long as his rent was current, he could care less but he did always wonder where he'd go in case he'd have to get rid of his stuff for a new renter.

"Hey Joe, where have you been the past few days?"

"Jail, David."

David is unconcerned but plays along anyway. "What happened? No wonder I didn't see you around. The Goal Crease staff called here, wondering where you were."

"Just a misunderstanding."

"You seem to have a lot of misunderstandings, Joe."

"Well, I did not really do anything, you know how I told you Rick has been out of town a few weeks?"

"Sure, why?"

"Well, he asked me to water his plants while he was away, so I said yes, of course I would. Then one day I was driving on Cape Coral Parkway and got pulled over and the cop asks me where I am coming from. And I tell him my buddy Rick's place, when he asks me what I was doing there? I innocently tell the police officer that my friend asked me to water his plants while he was away. Well, little did I know that was code for growing marijuana plants in some places. So, I got hauled down to the jail till this could get settled. Rick couldn't come back for a few days, so I had to wait till he got back."

"Why didn't you call me Joe?"

"I don't have your number, David, only your bank account number to make my rent payments."

"Jail, Joe, you must not have liked that too much."

"Naw, it wasn't too bad."

"Yeah, but I am sure a short, wiry, good-looking guy like you must have gotten some trouble, you know what I mean?"

"No, not really, I think most of the others were intimidated by me. No one seemed to bother me, my friend Bubba told them to be cool."

"Wow, you are lucky you did not get your ass kicked, Joe."

Joe holds his left hand against his backside. "Funny you should say that do you have any Tylenol around? My asshole is kind of sore, but I know nothing happened. I think it was because of having to sleep on those hard mattresses they give you."

David shakes his head in disbelief. "So, Rick finally got you out?"

"Yeah, finally, and just in time, the playoffs are starting soon, I didn't want to miss them."

32

Florida is the land of imagery and imagination, just look at the place with the mouse, right? Sometimes, one does not have to stray too far to have that kind of encounter.

Todd wanted to show Joe the wonders of a place nearby Fort Myers across a small causeway, Sanibel Island. For all Joe's goofiness and crazy antics he had gotten himself into, he was knowledgeable about some of the local scene, but even sometimes the line between reality and fantasy is blurred. He spotted a small place in Sanibel that he had heard about. After going to the beach and exorbitantly paying an outrageous hourly fee to just park his car, Joe convinces Todd to pull over at the place Joe had in mind.

"What are we doing at Doc Ford's Rum Bar & Grill, is it Happy Hour yet, Joe?"

"No, Todd, but since we're here, we might as well have a few cocktails. I came by to introduce myself to that guy named Doc Ford and get some scoops about things to do here in the area. He's a real guy I read about in those books by a local author."

Although Todd is not well read, he is aware of a local author that uses Sanibel as a backdrop for his fiction novels.

"Isn't he make believe, Joe?"

"No, Todd, why would someone name a few restaurants after a made-up character, besides, the stories are so real and describe real places. I heard he is usually here at this location in Sanibel about this time of day." Joe looks around anxiously trying to find someone, he even gets up from the bar and walks around the place. He finally gets the attention of a female bartender, makes a "come here" gesture to her and speaks in a whisper to her. "Miss, my name is Joe, Joe from Buffalo."

"Sorry to hear that, sir, how may I help you?"

"I was here hoping to meet that guy named Doc Ford who owns this place, oh wait that looks like him. Hey, Doc, Doc, got a minute?" Joe keeps talking as the man intentionally ignores him.

"Joe, he does not even acknowledge you, why do you think he is who you say he is?"

"Because of those pictures of him on the book covers, see?" Joe pulls out a half-ripped cover of a book and shows it to Todd, pointing at the illustration.

"This is a drawing, Joe, but yeah I do see the similarities."

"He must not like the attention and flattery of being a famous guy. Hey Doc, yoohoo?"

"I don't know maybe he's deaf, Joe."

The man insistently ignores Joe's catcalls. Joe talks louder to get the man's attention. "Hey, Doc, I just wanted to ask you a few things. Why is he ignoring me? I guess he thinks he's a hotshot."

The man finally relents and looks over at Joe and in an unmistakable British accent says, "Yes sir, and I can hear you, as annoying as it is. I have no idea of whom you speak of, I am a tourist enjoying this area."

"Oh, I get it, pretending to be like in the books, all mysterious and secretive, that dual role thing going on."

The bartender now scooches over closer to the patron. "Sir, is this man bothering you, do I need to get a manager or something?"

The man animatedly and emphatically gestures. "Yes, Miss, he keeps pestering me, thinking I am some Doc or something, I think he is drunk, too."

Todd attempts to mediate the now escalating discussion. "Hi Miss, my friend Joe here seems to think this guy is Doc Ford or something."

The bartender defends the man who is pulling away from this encounter with a belligerent Joe. "Doc Ford is a make-believe character, sir, why would you think this guy is him?"

Joe remains undaunted in his conviction. "You can't see the similarities between these book covers and this guy, this plays into his dual identity in the books, I was just trying to discuss some things of local interest to have new things to do here."

"Ma'am, I have no clue who this gentleman is speaking about, nor have I ever heard of Doc Ford other than the name of this fine culinary and beverage establishment."

Joe is red faced and beside himself now. "You think you can fool everyone Doc, I'm onto you."

"Come on Joe, let's go and not be an annoyance."

Again, as has happened numerous times now, a manager approaches Joe in a friendly way. "Sir, we have to ask you to leave because you are bothering one of our regular customers."

Joe screams out "Regular? Did you hear that, Todd? I knew that was him. Ok Doc, I'll just stop down at Dinkins Bay during one of your famous get-togethers. I'd rather meet Tomlinson than you anyway, he seems more tuned in than you, you phony."

Todd grabs Joe and pulls him out of the place to calm him down. "Well, Joe, you never fail to outdo even yourself, that was the first time we got kicked out of a place before we even had a drink, good job!"

33

Sometimes, you have got to take one for the team, or at the very least, talk someone else into taking one for the team. Florida is the spring training mecca for those snowbirds that need a break from the cold up north.

"The Minnesota Twins, really? I am not an AL Central fan; can't we do this at Jet Blue Park instead?"

"I told you, Joe, the Red Sox would never draft a Japanese player, Tung thinks he can get us into the Twins practice for free. Besides, it is a major league team, well, kinda."

"Hey, Todd, they won the World Series a few times."

"Yeah, back in the days of the Clinton presidency, maybe." Joe looks around anxiously wondering how they're going to pull this off. Sure, it's one thing to sneak into a minor league hockey game or avoid the cover charge at a bar but this is the Bigs. "So how is he going get us into these practices for free?"

"He is going to pretend to be a free agent prospect signed to be a relief pitcher."

"A 5'5" relief pitcher, oh that should work well."

"Come on, Joe, he is going to act like he cannot speak English at the gate, and we are his interpreters, you can be his agent."

"Me, an agent, an agent? I don't think so Todd."

"Ok, I'll be his agent, you be his interpreter and make a lot of hand signals like a 3rd base coach, they'll never know."

"Does Tung know where to go when we get inside the gate, he has to act like he knows where he is going, if we can even get away with this."

"You are such a pussy, Joe, just go with it, most of pulling it off is acting like we should be here."

"Well, I don't know, Todd."

Tung speaks up confidently. "Ah, Joe, we ah can do dis."

Joe is still unconvinced as he sees young families smiling as they enter the gates to the stadium. They are sitting in Joe's minivan at the entrance to the lot. "Yeah, but the Twins, Tung, can you even name a player on their roster?"

Todd pipes up, "No, so, Joe, you are the one that keeps saying you want to do Florida stuff, well, sneaking into a spring training game is definitely one of the must dos you should do."

"Ok, I am game, is there at least free parking? I don't have any cash, and besides, I can't stand paying to park."

"We know, Joe, that's why you park about 3 miles down the beach and we walk there instead of parking in a paid lot. Geesh, Joe, I will pay for the parking, but you get the first round of beers at the game."

As they approach the lot attendant, Joe says "Well, I went to an Everblades game and told the guy I was a little short on cash, and he said no problem, catch me next time. That's why I started liking the Florida Everblades, that is called good customer relations."

"Did you ever go back and settle up, Joe?"

"No, but that's not the point."

"Ok, here we are at the gate, Joe, can you do this at least to get us in?"

"Sure, Todd, but what happens if he somehow gets in the locker room?"

"Let me handle it."

"OK Todd, whatever you say."

Todd's plan surprisingly works when the regular locker room attendant that checks the players in gets a sudden stomach virus and runs to the bathroom and is in there an awfully long time. Todd takes the lead and tells another player that notices when Tung walks over to an open locker, that Tung was supposed to be there and was just signed about 15 minutes ago for a tryout.

The player shrugs and walks away. Todd sees Tung being outfitted in catcher's gear and shrugs his shoulders and goes back up into the stands. Tung is rattled and cannot understand what's going on and why he is wearing this silly outfit, but he wants to fit in with his new friends. He is told to follow the other players on to the practice field to practice for the game. He doesn't know what to do, or where to go until one of the other catchers shows him where to go. He looks through the crowd for his friends.

Todd and Joe are sitting comfortably but unnoticeable in the right field stands. "Hey, I guess this was a good idea, Todd, how cool getting to go in the locker and meet some of the players."

"They did not appreciate you taking a piss in the shower, Joe."

"What? I had to go really bad. Why is Tung dressed in a catcher's uniform, Todd?"

Todd acts surprised. "Hmmm, that looks like a catcher's outfit, I thought he said he was an infielder?"

Tung is completely out of place and has no idea what to do, when Joe notices him gesturing frantically.

"This is kind of cool here, looks like he is trying to tell them he is not a catcher, but they won't listen to him. Why are those guys forcing him to keep the catcher stuff on, Todd?"

"Maybe they know better than we do, he looks good in the equipment."

"Is he really going to go through with this?"

"I don't know but they won't let him change, so I guess so."

"Well, at least we had the experience to see the players up close and personal, that is cool."

"What about Tung though? He is probably going to get injured out there."

Tung is frantically pointing up in the stands in Todd and Joe's direction. "Oh well, that's the chance we take in life, he'll be ok."

"He keeps pointing at us, keep moving, act like we don't know him, besides, he has padding on, he will be ok."

Joe has a pang of sympathy for what Tung is about to go through. "Did you ever have Kyle Gibson throw a fastball at you Todd?"

"Eh, it can't be that bad, they finished 5th last season, they got him to home plate, at least, he looks pretty cool, like he fits in, I envy him, he has a great seat for this."

"I don't know, Todd, he still seems a little irritated."

"When I said this $100 was towards his share, he was all in, then, Joe, what can I say?"

Tung is completely lost and tries to recall his only experience in baseball, which was his participation once in his younger sister's softball game. He finally is behind the plate at the urging of the impatient umpire.

Joe sees Tung making what appears to be hand signals to the confused pitcher. "Is he trying to signal the pitcher, that looks real. I don't get it, the pitcher is running up to him, he does not seem so happy. Oh, was that a punch he threw at Tung? Tung deflected that well." Joe is commenting about the actions on the field to Todd, who is scoping the crowd for hot women fans. "Ok, the pitcher went back to the mound, they must be on the same page now." Joe talks in his Howard Cosell voice, not knowing or realizing Howard Cosell never did baseball as an announcer. The next pitch blows by Tung, him not even close to catching it or slowing it down even. "Oh wow, he did not even come close to catching that pitch, he dropped his glove and threw up his hands. At least it was a strike, the ump is asking him if he is ok."

The pitcher is obviously irritated with Tung's signals, almost as if he could not decipher the gestures, and wildly throws the ball at the highest velocity he could muster. The ball hits Tung squarely on the top of his catcher's mask and Tung reflexively goes down and doesn't move at all. "Ouch, that had to hurt, a ninety mile per hour fastball to his helmet, good pitch!" Tung is lying on the ground, on his back, looking completely unconscious.

"Chin music to your own catcher, that is low, Joe."

Joe loses interest and gets up to stretch out. "I need a beer Todd, this is fun, I never knew baseball could be so violent." Before he could get out of the aisle, more action occurs on the field. The pitcher rushes the mound as a disgruntled hitter would run towards the mound on a questionable pitch.

"Why is the pitcher attacking Tung, his own catcher, this is better than a hockey fight".

"I think Tung used the wrong hand signal, Todd, pitchers are so sensitive."

34

David is rummaging around the fridge for leftovers that Joe usually leaves and forgets about by the next day due to his drunkenness. Joe is walking by the kitchen on his way to his room, Joe giving a short, aggravated grunt to David.

"Why in a bad mood, Joe, what's up?"

"Well, you know how I have had to be cool about driving because of the suspended license, David?"

"Yeah, but you seem to drive a lot anyway, but go on."

"I know, man, and I have been riding my bike more, especially from the Goal Crease because it isn't too far, but get this, I got a ticket last night riding home from there."

"A ticket for bike riding, Joe, huh?"

"Yeah, for not using hand signs when I came to a stop, well actually I went through a stop sign and cop pulled me over, then he added no helmet, no flashing lights and said something about ignorant stupidity."

"Well, he probably wasn't that far off the mark, Joe and besides I told you they take their traffic laws down here seriously, this isn't the big city like where you come from."

"This is such BS, man, here I am a law-abiding white man trying to follow the laws and then this. I swear I have never had one ounce of trouble my whole life, and then in space of a few months I have been jailed, ticketed for a driving offense, now this. If I did not know any better, I'd say someone is out to get me."

"Well, this is a place that welcomes all kinds, maybe you just don't fit in anymore?"

35

What is more Florida than a day at the beach? Of course, Joe and his friends' definition of beach going is much different than most.

Joe has been able to breathe easier and not have to look behind his back so much these days, there have been no close calls with law enforcement, no strangers lurking in the background, but it has been a while since he's had any female interaction.

"I love coming down to the beach, Todd, it's like a mini vacation."

"Exactly, Joe, and right here at Fort Myers Beach is all you need, there's no need to go anywhere else."

"Yeah, especially because of that place that offers 99 cent drafts for happy hour."

"Rick said he'd meet us down here later, Tung said he'd be up soon, had a massage with a happy ending at one of those massage parlors down on 41."

Joe looked like he saw a ghost. "They have those here, Todd, why didn't you tell me? I love happy endings, especially from those Oriental chicks, they know how to please their man."

"Joe, every chick you seem to be with pleases you."

"Well, not that chick that jacked me at the river park, and I don't mean jacked off, though I wouldn't have minded that, even."

Todd foggily remembers Joe telling him about the supposed robbery attempt at the park down by the river where Joe was self-delusional about his purported conquest of that hot blonde from the Goal Crease. "Oh yeah, that was memorable, you sure know how to pick them, Joe."

Tung walks up in cargo pants, a mesh shirt and a Minnesota Twins cap. The team decided to make him an honorary member after his escapade of pretending to be a player, with the express condition that he no longer ever goes to the stadium or even visit an opposing team's stadium if the Twins are playing somewhere else.

"Oh, here comes Tung, all smiles, that guy is such a hound."

"Ah, Joe, and ah, Todd, where da young poosy at?"

Joe waves his hand at a completely empty beach front. "Dude, look around you, plenty of it." There is less than half a dozen folks on the beach, most of them retired.

"Ah no, I mean da young giwls, me like them young and fwesh."

Tung looks leery eyed at a teenaged girl and holds his tongue between forked fingers. The girl looks at him terrified and runs off immediately.

"Is this guy for real, what's he doing wagging his tongue at those girls, he might get arrested if he is not careful."

One of the other girls saw his sick demonstration looks back and giggles in a teasing way, winking at him.

"They seem amused and fascinated, I don't get it, Joe."

Joe puts on sunscreen, lays it thick on his nose and ears making it look like he is a lifeguard on the Bay Watch TV show, he thinks. "Hey, Todd, I wish I could pick up chicks like he does, well, older ones. But hell, I am so hard up at the moment, I'd even do a fat, toothless hunchbacked broad, oh wait, I have."

"Well, Joe, your chances would be greater if you didn't wear those faggy panties."

Joe looks down at his flower swim trunks and pats his tummy, it makes that hollow sound like an empty barrel. "Guess again, Todd. Oh, by the way, I asked Marissa to drop by and meet us later at Happy Hour".

"A second date for you, Joe, wow maybe there's hope for you after all."

"Well, I don't want to rush things with her, I can't put a finger on it, but I know I don't want to just have sex with her to just do it like a conquest or something. Like I said before, there is something different about her and I can't put a finger on it exactly, it's just that I don't want this to be a wham, bam, thank you ma'am thing with her. In the meantime, it never hurts to check out the scenery."

After about a half hour of sitting on his towel and getting up a few times, Joe suggests they head over to happy hour. It is barely 11 in the morning. Todd starts to instinctively follow Joe to the bar on the beach that has the early happy hour.

"Is it almost happy hour, I'm thirsty. Hey where's Tung going, he's going to miss out." Tung looks at the guys, a devilish smile on his face.

"Uh, I ah go to woom wit dis chick and do her doggystyle and othew ways, I no can wait to hear her bawk wike a dawg, woof woof."

"I dunno, Tung, are you sure it's cool, she looks awfully young."

"Hey, miss, how old are you?"

The obviously underaged girl twirls her hair at the question and stutters a second. "I, I, am 18 or so, why, I am old enough."

"So, what year were you born in, answer me that."

"Around the beginning of the century, I think, why?"

"What do you mean, as in 2000 or something?"

"Something like that, yeah."

"Ok, have fun. Ah, young love is there anything more romantic?" Joe waves bye to the happy couple, Tung holding his arm around the girl and whisks her away quickly before she has a change of heart.

"I need a drink, it's been a long day, Joe, did you see Rick around yet, he's going to miss the 99 cent drafts."

At that moment, the guys spot Rick trudging along the beach, red as a lobster that has been boiled, looking like he is in agony.

"Oh, here he comes, hey Rick, what's up, why do you have those welts on your legs?"

"Eh, I had an unfortunate run in with an overzealous, focused jellyfish, this sucker stings. Are the beers still 99 cents? I need to take away the pain."

Todd runs up to his buddy in genuine concern and unzips his shorts to urinate on his stunned friend's feet, he thinks he is helping him out. Rick is stunned and does not know what to say. "Todd, what are you doing, why did you pull your dick out, dude, we're in public, what the hell you doing?"

"Relax, Rick, this will help take the sting out of the jellyfish bite, human urine is the best cure, it's cool."

"I don't need no golden shower, pal, put that thing away or there is going to be some major urinary tract problems for you in the future."

"Geesh, buddy, I was just trying to help a pal out of a bind."

36

Make no mistake about it, one of the real appeals to Florida is the warm water surrounding it, making it a chosen destination of many everywhere. For some, it only serves as another purpose or place to push the limits.

In looking to find even new and different things to do there, Joe discovers a cheesy Pirate Ship tour complete with a fake cannon and crumbling plastic crow's nest. The guys have reasonably settled on the replica ship, Joe has not broken anything yet. Even though the others complained about dressing up to play their parts on this tourist-driven excuse for real life adventures, they succumbed to Joe's whining to play along so they came dressed up in their own unique pirate garb.

"I like the eyepatch, fake beard and Star Wars Light Sabre sword as your costume, Jeremy, you look like a real swash buckling pirate." Joe yanks on the overgrown scruffy beard, pinching Jeremiah's face.

"Get your hands off me." Jeremiah, in reflex reaction, swats at Joe. "My beard's not fake, John."

"It's Joe, dude, and what do you mean it's not real, I thought the 'Red Beard' thing was taking it a little far, but ok."

"Just because you are wearing a striped shirt, bandana, fake wooden leg and a plastic parrot on your shoulder doesn't make you more a pirate than me, besides, I think you look stupid in that outfit."

Joe has even gone so far has to shed his usual apparel of floral pattern swim trunks and striped shirt in the spirit of this trip. He points over his left shoulder at Todd, who just came up to them. "Aw, get into the spirit, Jeremy, it will be fine, in fact look at Todd over there dressed up as a Johnny Depp look alike from 'Pirates of the Caribbean', now he has embraced the spirit of this trip in true fashion. Of course, it is not too flattering that his belly button is popping out from under his NY Rangers jersey, but the Rangers eyepatch is a nice touch."

"He doesn't look like Johnny Depp, he looks more like a scary Phyllis Diller, not a swash buckling pirate."

Joe looks around anxiously. "I wonder where Rick is, he said he'd meet us here, he always seems to be running late to these things."

Rick meets them in his usual dress for special occasions, his cowboy outfit with shit kicker boots. Jeremiah spots him and highlights his incorrect outfit for the event. "And there's Rick in his cowboy boots, shorts, cowboy hat and polka dot bandana."

Joe is surprised by Rick's outfit, he told Joe he'd come in appropriate attire for a ship, not the dang rodeo.

"What, why did he come like that? Hey, Rick, I told you it was a Pirate Ride, not a cowboy ride."

Rick looks down at himself as he acts like he is surprised by his choice. "What, oh, I did not have a pirate outfit, besides I bet at some point somewhere a cowboy has ridden on a pirate ship before so what's the big deal?"

Joe shakes his head and changes the subject. He knows Rick has been very delayed in his efforts to remodel the formerly Chinese dry walled home he picked up for a song in Cape Coral. "Meant to ask you Rick, how's the place coming along?"

"Not too well, at the moment, Joe, seems like the place was built over a sinkhole, now my living room is a real 'sunk in' living room."

"Cool Rick, that's like a place where a movie star would live, how cool is that?" Joe nods his head in approval and doesn't seem to understand what Rick's really telling him. "I hear they have Pirate karaoke; I already saw the list of songs and I chose Donna Summer's Dancing Queen; it was either that or Billy Ocean's Caribbean Queen, in honor of the trip, but I think I can pull off Donna Summer easier."

Todd hiccups and speaks up loud enough for others to hear him. "Are you sure you're not gay, Joe?"

"Why would you say that, Todd? Donna Summer rose above most gender boundaries, God rest her soul. Just between you and I though, I think she was actually a dude in drag. She was a diva long before these pseudo modern divas were even born!" "Do they have Budweiser on here?"

"No, only Sapporo."

Joe is unaware of his offensive language. "Isn't that a chink beer?"

Todd reciprocates. "No, Jap one, I think."

"Damn, Orientals are even taking over tourism here, for God's sakes, is anything sacred?"

"Here, here, let's have a few shots of Captain Morgan to get us in the mood for the trip."

Jeremiah is playing with something in his hands, looks like a rubber ball. The boat has not even left the dock yet and Todd looks around bored already.

"So, what else is there to do on the boat, Joe, other than get plowed and listen to your horrendous version of Dancing Queen?"

Joe tries to perk up Todd. "I heard they have a treasure hunt, that should keep Rick busy. Todd walks off in a huff, and mingles with the others, mostly tourists from the Midwest who never were on water of any type. A certain, much older, partially blind school-teacher type is all over Todd, who looks like he is trying to shoo her away. "Hey, maybe that Johnny Depp outfit is working for Todd, looks like he has a fan club, lucky guy." Jeremiah sees Todd's apparent disinterest in her and overhears the smitten lady's comments about The Wizard of Oz.

"Um, sure, Joe, if you think he will go for that retired schoolteacher type, and that's not a costume she's wearing, I think she really is like 70 or something and keeps hitting on him, telling him she liked him better in the Wizard of Oz, personally I thought that was a piece of crap."

"Hey Jeremy, schoolteachers can be hot, you know what I mean?"

"No, Jack, I don't.

"You remember that Van Halen song Hot for Teacher, Jer?"

Jeremiah is sick of Joe's inane, useless blubbering about mindless pop culture, especially some band from a long time ago, way past their prime. He had come on here hoping to stage an 'accidental" mishap involving Joe, but he had to make sure it was clean and simple. Just then he snapped back into the conversation.

"Van who, oh you mean that band touring now that wears sickeningly tight spandex pants thinking they're still young guys, the fat, overaged, bald dudes that can't sing for a crap? They could not even sing in their prime from what I saw on YouTube."

A loud boom erupts disrupting their discussion. "Whoa, what was that noise, Joe?"

"Oh, that was a fake cannon they shoot at the Beach goers as a goof."

Just then, Jeremiah's mood and personality change instantly. Jeremiah raises what appears to be a fake machete toy he wore with his costume and swings it by Joe so closely he can hear the swooshing air as it misses him. He thought he saw a real glitter in the sword part of it, it seemed real, not fake to Joe.

"I'll have none of that Joe, I think there's a mutiny going on, I'm gonna find the culprit and make him walk the plank, arrrgggggg! I thought this was gonna be a relaxing trip, I can't get away from my job ever." Jeremiah is relieved to not have to deal with Joe and his stupid questions and runs out of sight.

"You do that Jeremy; I have to find Rick and Todd."

"Hey Todd, did you see Rick around, he's going to miss my karaoke singing."

"I think I saw him with a pickax heading below." Joe shakes his head and laughs heartily. "That Rick is a character, I wonder how he got a hold of a fake pickax, I knew he'd take this treasure search seriously. "

Just then, Rick yells excitedly to the guys. "Hey guys, I found where "X" marks the spot for the treasure." Rick leads them to the bottom level on the boat and excitedly points to the "X" spray painted in silver on the bottom.

"Oh, you mean from the preprinted glossy map they give you when we came aboard?"

"What map are you talking about, Joe, I never saw a map, I found this on my own, I think I found the treasure. I need this to fund my next half year of trips to "Coochie Ha Has strip club." Rick takes a few swings of the ax and aims at the "X."

"Rick, what are you doing, is that thing real?"

"Yeah, of course it is. Uh oh, I think I hit the wrong thing with this axe, why is that water coming in here?" The axe hits the bottom causing a small hole at the bottom of the boat, the water trickling slowly at first, then starting to pour in the boat more and more.

"Quick, Rick, I think we have to get out of here."

Just then a bellowing horn comes on and the crowd panics, bodies flying everywhere to get off this sinking ship. Joe, Rick, and Todd somehow make their way up to the main deck and look over at Jeremiah, who is herding the others to the fake makeshift plank, holding his machete over them and forcing them to jump off the plank. He was not aware that there was a genuine emergency on the boat at that moment.

"Alas matey, man overboard."

"Why is Jeremiah making those folks walk the fake plank? He's actually forcing people to abandon the ship."

"Good thing, because I think she's going down anyway after what Rick did."

37

The gang did not see each other for a few days after the Pirate ship fiasco but eventually Joe wanders over to The Goal Crease to think about the other day. He sees Todd in the usual spot, it is a bit earlier than usual for him, but Joe had other things on his mind. Even though he did not outwardly show it, he got spooked a bit when Jeremiah playfully swiped at Joe with the machete, it did not look like a play toy one, it looked real.

"Hey, Todd, how's it going, that was a fiasco the other day on the pirate ship. I am glad the Coast Guard came along and saved the day."

"Yeah, we were pretty lucky, most of the people were forced off by Jeremiah anyway so they were wading in the water already."

"How about Rick, what happened to him?"

"Well, he won the treasure contest, thing is the prize was a free trip on a future excursion, the bad thing is, he has to replace the boat."

"Damn that's harsh, the whole boat was a cheap replica anyway. The main deck, berth, bilge, and crows' nests were pretty flimsy, probably assembled in China."

Todd shakes his head in agreement but has something else on his mind too. "So, Joe, I was at a few joints down on the beach and I don't know how you managed to do it, but your picture is prominently displayed on a NOT ALLOWED poster and I heard that there are more posters being printed for places you have not even gone in yet."

Joe feels he is being singled out by everybody. "Hey, I can't help no one has the same unique, witty sense of humor I have, besides, their loss, beer sales will be decreasing at those places, I guess. I bring a lot of business, referrals, all that."

Todd plays along with it. "Yeah, Joe, whatever you say, old buddy."

Joe changes the subject immediately to forget all this nonsense of banishment from places. "Anyway, you know what I wonder, Todd?"

"Oh no, ok I'll bite, what do you wonder about?"

"Funny you should say bite, you know how they serve gator bites here at The Goal Crease?"

"Yeah...."

"How would we know if they are gator or crocodile?"

Todd emits a sigh of relief, realizing he will not be dragged into some meaningless petty conversations about huge hooters on chicks or anything shallow.

"Oh, it's definitely gator, I am told crocodile has a fishy taste to it."

"That makes sense, so not a chicken taste, I mean it could be rabbit or squirrel even, how would we know it is gator?"

"Because it says so on the menu, why would they lie? It's kind of like those Chinese places if it says it's chicken, it's chicken, I guess?"

"I heard sometimes they serve rat though, now that would be false advertising."

"Well, anyway Joe, thanks to you we are running out of places to go and drink, although we have not hit the casino yet."

"I heard drinks are way too much there, besides, they're Mexican owned and I don't support foreign interests."

"No, they're not Joe, they are Native American owned, not Mexican."

"Oh, well they all look alike to me, Mexicans, Indians, this place is going to hell in a hand basket."

"So, do you want to go to the casino, Joe, you have not been banned there yet."

"Do they have karaoke there, I can do "Cherokee Nation." Joe tries to cheer up and forget his woes.

"No, but they have trivia, like who was the first NY Ranger to appear in the very first NHL All Star Game in 1931?"

"Um, I don't know Todd, Lester Patrick?"

"Nope, Bill Cook, of course."

"I cannot imagine we will ever hear that question in a trivia quiz here in SW Florida but hey, you never know, speaking of hockey, you know the Skate–ATerium is open all year round to ice skate, even here in Florida. We should get the guys together for a pickup game sometime."

"I haven't played in years, Joe, I might be a little rusty."

Joe had someone in mind he wanted to get even with, that showed him up on his home turf, The Goal Crease. "That's ok, maybe we can get Kris Draper to join us?"

38

Joe is spending a quiet day in his room, tidying up his little space when he sees his roommate in the garage where he is usually puttering around, reorganizing his potato chip collection. A few rabid mosquitoes are buzzing around, David slapping his face and body to rid the swarming mosquitoes. He looks up at Joe who stepped in to use the washer.

"So, what's hap'n Cap'n?"

"Not much, David, have a date with a cutie later, just want to get a few things done before."

"Oh really, what's his name?" David amuses himself at his lame attempt at humor.

"It's not a guy, silly, it's a Puerto Rican chick."

"Uh oh, I hear they are wild in bed Joe, you better be careful, she might cut you."

"I know, I was with her the other night."

David is dismayed that he might have missed meeting this chick here at the house and get a listen to her noise levels during sex. "Where did you do that, I did not hear you the other night like the other times."

Joe ignores his comments. "Get this, David, she was staying overnight at a hospital, and she asked me to come up after I got off from work."

David knows from Joe's routines and habits when his shifts at the gas station start and when they end about 9 p.m. and Joe usually stops by The Goal Crease for a few. "You went up that late, didn't they have visiting hours?"

"I don't know, I walked right up, and no one said anything. So, we are in her room, and she walks over to the door and shuts it, then pulls me to the bed and we start to go at it, when she notices my unusual under garments. Then she says, you wear women's panties, and oh look, bunnies on them, that is so hot, what a turn on, blah blah, blah. Then she says, 'fuck me right this minute!' She pulls her hospital gown down and she is completely naked under it, I never realized patients are like that. She contorts her body in ways I never saw before, and she uses her mouth to unzip my pants."

David looks down on his wrist, pretending to look at a watch that does not rest on his wrist. "Does this story have an ending, Joe? I just got a new batch of chips in and there is a rare Frank Sinatra one in it, with his hat on."

"She was wild and was even yelling, I had to put my hand over her mouth to keep her quiet, but she kept biting my hand, so I was screaming too. I think the nurses heard us and one came in while I was doggy styling her, and the nurse just said 'oh my', and closed the door. No fricking privacy in hospitals no more, damn shame. She told me she was being released this morning and wanted to continue what we started but I insisted on showing her the happy hour down at the beach, and then we can get to it. Catch ya later, I am meeting her and driving down to the beach for happy hour."

39

Joe pulls up to the hospital entrance in his van to pick up Sarah. He is wearing his usual beach outfit, floral patterned swim trunks and striped shirt and cap.

Sarah comes out in tiny skintight shorts, a tan very low-cut tank top and jumps into the van. "I like the ride, Joe, where's the mattress in the back that are usually in vans like this?"

She bites her lip and looks over her shoulder, but Joe is oblivious to the obvious intention of Sarah. He can't wait to show her the place down at the beach that has 99 cent drafts for Happy Hour. On the way to the beach, Joe loses his direction and is anxious to not lose valuable time at Happy Hour. He knows from past experience that the place strictly follows the time and literally, a minute after Happy Hour, prices triple or more! Meanwhile, Sarah is playing with the back of Joe's neck and occasionally reaches over to tongue his ear. Joe swats at her playfully to stop. He is on a mission to get to the beach in a timely manner. Luckily, Joe finds that there is an open free parking space next to the place and he hastily gets Sarah out of the vehicle, and they get a seat on the patio overlooking the Gulf.

"You look so hot, Sarah. Are you sure you want a few drinks; you said you don't drink. I don't want to get you in trouble."

"Oh no, it's fine, Joe, besides it gets me horny."

Joe looks up and spots a server and snaps his fingers. "Waitress, we'll have another pitcher of margaritas with extra tequila, immediately, please."

The server looks blankly at Joe and goes to help another customer.

Sarah is uninterested in getting any drinks at all, she just wants to have sex as soon as possible. "You know you want me, Joe, you know how us Puerto Rican chicks are."

"Yeah, I do know, after the other night, I never had anyone do that upside down like you did."

The server finally drops off the pitcher of margaritas and a couple frosted mugs. Sarah puts her fingers in the drink, then sips on her drink, and puts her fingers in Joe's mouth. "You know you want me, Joe." "Unh unh, you want me more, Sarah," Joe says playfully. He notices Sarah looking down at her watch. "Why are you looking at your watch so much, Sarah, are you in a hurry?"

"My husband's going to be home around 3."

"What, you're married, you never told me!"

"It never came up, Joe, last night or today, what, are you afraid of my husband?"

"But you had your profile on a dating site, what's up with that?"

"Yes, and if you read it instead of only looking at the pictures of my huge tits, you would have seen I listed attached in the relationship status."

Joe pauses and takes a drink of the margarita, smacking his lips. "You people are a little too liberal down here, though that was a great time the other night, I gotta admit. I never did it in a hospital room. Are you sure you should be slamming another pitcher of margaritas when you have to be home in an hour, I am a little uncomfortable with this."

Sarah runs her one hand along Joe's chest, running her fingers from the other hand to the tip of her bountiful boobs. "You want it too; you know you do."

"Well, it was pretty incredible when you were screaming in the hospital room the other night." Oddly, Joe is starting to get turned on and now wants to get with her quickly before he must take her home to her husband. Joe throws a wad of money on the table in anticipation of what's going to happen next, he hopes.

Sarah gets up from her chair, woozily. "I am feeling a little tipsy, Joe, can you hold on to me walking down these stairs, I feel a little woozy." Sarah does a flip and tumbles down the stairs headfirst including a complete turnaround flip crashing against the sidewalk at the bottom of the stairs. Joe was partially distracted when a gorgeous woman in a revealing bikini top was walking up the stairs as he was helping Sarah traverse them.

"Oops, honey, I'm so sorry, you moved too fast, and you slipped out of my arms, and I got distracted by that hot chick on the stairs, sorry, are you ok?"

"No, I'm in pain, my head hurts, do I look ok to you?" She looks up laughing, a large red welt protruding in the middle of her forehead.

"Let me see that, it doesn't look too bad, he'll never notice these bruises on your face, he probably hits you anyway, I hear those Latin men are pretty hot headed. Let's get you to the van and get you back."

Sarah corrects Joe's assumptions. "He's Polynesian, not Puerto Rican. I get so turned on when I'm in pain, Joe let's just have a quickie here, no one will notice."

All of a sudden, Joe is consciously aware of his location and looks around worriedly. "But we are in a public parking lot in mid-day, someone might see us." Joe is worked up at this point, not sure what to do.

"You know you want these; you've been staring at them all day." Sarah lifts her tank top up, revealing her massive mounds, tiny hard dark nipples, with large aereolas, Joe can't contain himself anymore.

"Don't pull your shirt up here, damn, those do look good, maybe a little taste." He relents to the temptation and starts to suckle them ferociously.

"Yes, Joe, suck on them, makes me feel so good."

"You Puerto Rican chicks are horny all the time, aren't you?"

"Mmmmm, shut up, just keep sucking, Joe."

Joe suddenly feels a presence nearby, like when one encounters it as they are at a stoplight in their car. A small girl looks curiously in the van, seeing two figures in close quarters in the passenger front bucket seat, when she points at them.

"Mommy, why is that man kissing that lady's chest?"

The woman shrieks in abject horror and throws her hands immediately over her daughter's eyes, slapping her husband violently on his shoulder.

"Huh, Jessica?"

"Oh my God, George, say something."

George himself caught quite an eyeful and was admiring Sarah's display of womanhood. He makes a half-hearted attempt to stop this couple. "Hey, don't do that, stop sucking on her tits, hey, that is wrong Mister. Oh well, I tried to stop them dear, but she does have nice tits, what do you want me to say?"

The family slinks away in horror. Joe looks over at the departing family, then goes back to Sarah's exposed boobs. "Please Sarah, we have to stop, I think that kid just saw us."

"I think her daddy enjoyed the show, so what?"

"Yeah, but mommy looks pissed."

Sarah disgustedly pushes Joe off her. "Ok, we can go now, Joe, I need to sleep this off before he gets home anyway."

40

The guys decided to have a fun filled action packed night. It would start at the local minor league hockey game and ensue in a night of debauchery at the place near to the arena right after.

Tung had attached himself nicely to the group and participated in most of their group activities, besides, even though he said he was a hockey fan, he had never been to a game. Todd was smart enough to realize that they would all go if there was a reason, and two-dollar beer, one-dollar hot dog night was that reason. As usual, Joe overdid it, got obnoxiously drunk and even yelled so loud that the other fans could hear his taunting chants at the poor mascot. For some reason, the ushers and management let this unruly action go. It was hard enough to just get anyone into the games and spend money, one guy would not ruin it for all the others, right? Jeremiah joined the group even though he had other pressing matters, but if he saw a chance to get his dirty deed done, then so be it. The game got out of control and the score was one sided, so they decided to head over to the place nearby. It was a cool place and had games there including a shuffleboard game, a table one where you threw metal disks into the scoring triangle.

Jeremiah saw his chance, maybe he could take out Joe and make it look like an accident? He was good at this game and was accurate he thought. He would propose a 4-player set up, two of them on one side, two on the other but he had to get Joe on the opposite side to make this happen. He finally gets a few others to play and gets the right lineup. Tung did not want to play so he decided he'd play the jukebox, he wanders over to it and plays awful music that Joe does not want to hear, so he leaves the table and catches Tung just before he gets to the jukebox and asks him to hold his place, that Joe could pick out better songs. Tung goes over to the table to wait for Joe, but Joe is nowhere to be found. Joe remembered just then that he had to make a call to his aunt, one thing led to another, he got tired and decided to head home.

The next day, Todd calls him on his cell.

"Hey, Joe, where did you go last night, you'll never believe what happened after you left the bar after the Blades game. Tung died."

"Huh, what, how, he seemed ok when I left. I was tired when I left, oh wow."

"Yeah, you know that shuffleboard table there. We were playing a couple games, and Jeremiah was taking a shot, Tung was over at the jukebox looking at the list of songs."

"Did he pick out any good ones at least, he has the worst taste in music, you ask me."

Todd continues. "So, there he is hunched over by the jukebox, Jeremiah whizzes the puck down the table, it flies right off the table, almost hard as a Bobby Hull slapshot, hits him square in the temple and drops him like a bag of pucks. Never seen anything like it."

Joe remains unconcerned or even cognizant of what Todd just told him. "Did you at least win the game, Todd?"

"Yeah, and the worst part was, because of his unfortunate demise, he welched on his bet with Jeremiah."

Joe heard Rick in the background. "That's ok, we're good, he had a few bucks in his wallet, we're all good."

"I hope he had enough to cover his bet at least."

41

Patrick and Jeremiah arrive on time for tee time at the golf course. Jeremiah has a special surprise for Joe. He booby trapped some golf tees for Joe that would explode on impact when the club strikes the tee. They had the impact and power of those pipe bombs you see on the news that can wipe out a block over in the Middle East somewhere. Oh well if Patrick is taken out too, collateral damage, what can you do, thought, Jeremiah? It would look completely like an accident, an unfortunate coincidence that Joe grabbed the wrong tees at the wrong time and is the victim of some horrendous prank meant for someone else. The only thing Jeremiah had to do was slip the rigged tees in Joe's bag when he wasn't looking. That would be easy, Joe usually had to take a leak every hole or so, and Jeremiah ensured that fact by packing a case of Buds in his own golf bag. He also had the presence of mind to rig these special tees that formed into topless girls, knowing full well Joe's dispensation for such hokey, stupid items like that. God, Joe was such a simpleton, he'd go for anything.

"Where's Joe at, he said he'd be here at starting time. I told him when we were going out, I wanted to show him my new set of clubs."

"Relax, Patrick, he's usually pretty prompt though I have to say he is usually waiting for us whenever we do anything, especially when it involves alcoholic beverages. I have a case of Buds in my bertha bag, it doesn't look too obvious, does it?" He points to his overstuffed golf bag on a two-wheel cart, the wheels deflated and flat from the weight of the contents of it.

"Naw, Jeremiah, it looks like a cave for a small family of bears, but no, it's not too noticeable. How did you fit all of them in there anyway?"

"I took most of the clubs out, I only need a wood, a five iron and putter pretty much."

"That sounds about right, you can drive it pretty far, maybe get on the greens in a shot or two anyway."

The guys look over at the parking lot looking for signs of the ancient silver wood grained minivan.

"Well, looks like he isn't going to make it in time, guess we'll just start without him."

Jeremiah is starting to get anxious and impatient. He tries to stall them at the first tee but there is no sign of Joe anywhere. What an idiot that Joe is, thought Jeremiah, he can't even be prompt to his own demise.

The foursome behind the guys is now starting to say things and even though they could let them go ahead, Patrick and Jeremiah decide to start. Jeremiah gives up hope that this would be Joe's final day here in paradise on Earth. Jeremiah is not known to skimp on sporting equipment and accessories and Patrick notices the expensive golf balls Jeremiah is using.

"Nice balls, Jeremiah."

Jeremiah is distracted. "Thanks, I'd like to think they do the job. Oh, you mean these new Titleist Titanium core ones. Yeah, guaranteed to increase length by at least 2 times. That's what it said on the late-night infomercial. You should have seen the knockers on the pitch woman, she could sell me anytime. They even included these tees that look like strippers, see the boobies on these."

"Wow, nice set of tees, Jeremiah."

Jeremiah was careful enough to separate the rigged tees from his own. He himself kind of liked the tees. He lines up his first shot and smashes the ball with fierce velocity, almost angrily. Jeremiah imagined Joe's head was the golf ball and that is why he crushed it.

"Wow, Jeremiah, awesome drive off the tee, you crushed it, I wish I could hit it that far off the tee."

Jeremiah puffs his chest out proudly, admiring his shot. "Well, when you are as active and fit as I am, and have the type of job I have, it keeps you limber and alert at all times."

"But wait, I thought you were a regional pharmaceutical sales rep or something, what kind of physical labor would you be doing on the job?"

"You'd be surprised, those druggies, er, patients are very demanding, no talk about work, ok Patrick? I am trying to relax and forget the job for a bit."

The two play out the first hole and get the scorecard from Patrick's cart.

"You beat me pretty good on that first hole, but this second hole is tricky with that water right here off the tee."

"Yeah, it's only 50 feet or so off the tee, no problem to get over it." Jeremiah puts the ball on his tee like the first hole and pulls out his wood, he is very confident. He winds up and makes minimal contact on the ball, the ball rolls 50 feet or so and goes in the water. Plop...... He is embarrassed but gains his senses and writes it off to a temporary loss of concentration. "Damn, I didn't see that coming, just get another ball." Jeremiah again puts another ball on his tee, puts his hands over his eyes making the appearance of checking how far the hole is from the tee. He slowly approaches the ball, winds up with his hands tightly on the club, blaming Joe in his mind for that bad shot. The ball this time comes off the tee in an arc, but it goes about 100 feet straight up and lands in the pond again. Plop...... He is determined to take this shot no matter what. He angrily grabs another ball from his bag. "Might as well tee up again." ....plop "Damn! This time I am going to get over the water" ... plop "I am getting pissed now, I am not giving up, giving up is for losers and unnecessary deaths result."... plop.

"I am surprised, Jeremiah. You hit that first shot a mile, this should be a piece of cake."

Jeremiah finally connects on this shot and Patrick yells out, 'four.'

"Why did you yell fore so loud, it's not like the ball went that far, no one's even around and I was not going to get hit or something."

"No, I yelled four, as in four shots now before we even get off the tee, Jeremiah."

They completed the play on this hole and Patrick is pretty sure he won the hole. Like many other golfers, there was a side bet between the competitors to buy each other a round of drinks at the bar later based on the lower score per hole.

"I shot a 4 this hole, Jeremiah, what did you shoot?"

Jeremiah without hesitation repeats, "same score."

"Huh, what about the first 6 shots that ended up in the water?"

Jeremiah is undeterred in his conviction of his score on the hole. "Those did not count, those were only practice shots, besides my cousin cleans the pond out and resells the balls. I was just trying to help a family member. Have you no heart, Patrick?"

Instead of arguing the point, Patrick grudgingly writes a four on the scorecard and the two continue on to the 3rd tee. As Patrick is cleaning his balls at the wash station, he hears a whisper.

"Pssssst, Patrick."

He sees Joe between the trees, his silhouette looking like a comic strip character in the Sunday funnies. Joe is wearing his usual outfit of flower-patterned swim trunks and striped shirt, but this time with goofy striped golf shoes. They could have been mistaken for bowling shoes.

"Joe, what are you doing in the trees, or should I even bother to ask? Lord knows what you would be humping out here."

"I was a little short of cash to play a full round so I thought I'd sneak on the course." "Well, you are short, that's for sure, but it is only 20 bucks, I would have paid for you."

"I appreciate that but that would take away from your beer money to buy mine at The Goal Crease later."

By the way, did Jeremy bring the beer?"

Jeremiah perks up and sees Joe talking to Patrick. "It's Jeremiah, don't you know my name by now?"

"Sorry, it's a mental thing."

"I'll say that again, Joe, just bring your clubs, come on, let's go."

Now that the moron Joe is here, now what, how do I get these tees into his bag without arousing suspicion, Jeremiah thinks?

Joe eagerly gets his stuff and starts to tee up his ball first.

"So, who is up first, my buddy told me there is a gator on this course. I sure would not want to hit a shot by it."

Patrick had played the course before and was familiar with the terrain and obstacles. "I heard it is on hole 8, Joe."

"Ok, maybe I will skip that hole, my roommate told me about a guy who lost his leg out here. I think that is a 'hole lie'."

Joe starts to line up his shot and does not notice he is aiming at the hole that Jeremiah and Patrick had just completed.

"Joe, why are you hitting back towards the hole we just got off?"

"Oops, I thought that was the flag for this hole, me bad." Joe makes what sounds like a perfect connection on his first shot, the ping of it sounding great. "That sounded like a great shot, where did it go?" Joe lost sight of the shot in the direct sun.

"Nice shot, Joe, the ball went straight and really high for only going about 20 yards off the tee, nice arc on the ball though. I thought you said you played before?"

"I did, last time was when Clinton was in office, but that counts. Besides, this is like riding a bicycle, it is not like you forget how to play".

The guys play ahead of Joe as they look back and shake their heads as the ball dribbles a few yards each shot. They decide to have a beer while waiting for Joe to finish the hole. Joe sees they are sipping a beer and he wants to join them.

"Wait up guys, at least I am on the green now."

"Yeah, Jeremiah and I finished this hole 10 minutes ago, seemed like you took 50 shots".

Joe finally sinks the putt and hastily joins the guys for a beer. The trio play a few more holes and Jeremiah and Patrick are now used to the slow pace and rhythm by now. Joe is still hitting the ball a few yards per shot. In the meantime, Jeremiah is getting aggravated because he cannot find a spot to plant the tees in Joe's bag. He would openly offer them to him, but again, Patrick or someone else might be suspicious so he bides his time waiting for the right moment. Patrick notices that Joe is having even more difficulty than usual on this hole and sees Joe hitting the ball on the green.

"Joe, why are you using that chipper on the green instead of a putter?"

"Oh, is that what this club is, I thought it was a putter. No wonder the ball isn't going anywhere when I hit it".

Joe continues to use the chipper despite Patrick's observation. He did not want to walk back and grab the right club. Joe finally finishes the hole and is parched.

"I need a beer, I'll get better next hole after I have a few more beers in me, I promise I'll get in the groove."

The skies are bright blue, the sun is out, no wind to speak of an otherwise perfect day for golf if you are a normal player.

"This is so relaxing, guys, isn't it?

"Depends on your definition of relaxing, if taking 20 minutes per hole is relaxing, then sure we'll go with that, but I don't think that foursome of octogenarians behind us are all that thrilled."

Joe looks around and sees four very upset, red-faced gentlemen in tweed shorts, checkered shirts, dapper bonnets and plaid socks behind them. "What, those guys? They are like in their 80's, what's their rush, they're gonna die sooner than us anyway. I would not be in a rush if I were them."

"It's called courtesy, Joe."

"Well, the guys ahead of us are not being courteous, they are two holes ahead of us now."

"Just shoot, Joe, geesh."

"Wait, I gotta take a piss, you know what they say about beer, we only rent it for a while. Where is the toilet?"

"Just go in the trees, come on, these guys are getting pissed."

"Fuck them if they can't relax like the rest of us. Everybody talks about how great this game is, I don't get it."

"We'll see you in about 15 minutes at the green Joe. Try to take less than 50 shots, this hole, ok?"

"What, I'm just getting my money's worth and using my full array of clubs, I want to get my money's worth."

"He does realize he didn't pay a cent to play, doesn't he, Jeremiah?"

As was the case before, Joe is nowhere to be found. The guys survey the course from their vantage point and can't see a whisk of Joe anywhere.

"Now where's Joe, Patrick? We should just keep moving and leave him behind." Jeremiah is beyond frustrated, knowing today will not be Joe's final day. Not only that, what could have been a relaxing calm day is now a shit show thanks to this idiot, Joe.

Just then, Patrick points like a pointer dog over on the green. "Oh, wait, Jeremiah, it looks like he is there, by the green." Joe is lying flat on his stomach in the middle of the green, his club by his side.

Patrick notices there is no one around and sees an idle ball on the green by Joe. "Oh look, a ball! I love finding balls on the course, it's like a special treat you don't expect. He looks passed out, maybe we should just let him rest awhile and come back for him after we're done?"

"I don't know, don't you think others will wake him up, or steal his clubs or something, Jeremiah?"

"If we're lucky, sure. Well, ok, let's let that foursome go ahead of us anyway."

The four older gentlemen grumpily proceed, one even spitting on Joe's lifeless body. Patrick swears he heard an Irish curse hurled at his buddy too and apologizes for his strange friend's odd playing style and habits.

"After you gentleman. It looks like our friend is out of action for now anyway, we won't be in your way anymore. Nice guys, everyone is so friendly on this course," says Patrick sarcastically.

They finish the round and are about to put their clubs in the car when Joe woozily wanders up to them, holding his head.

"Sorry you could not stay awake the whole round, Joe, you looked tired anyway."

"That's ok, at least I got my money's worth and got a few holes in."

"You did take more shots on those few holes than most people that play the whole course usually take, so yeah, I guess you did get your money's worth."

"My head kind of hurts, is this bump on my forehead that noticeable?" Joe grimaces and holds the top of his head.

"It ain't that bad, Joe."

"Thanks, any beer left? I need a few beers while I am relaxing out here on the course, makes me play better. We have to get out again, hopefully I'll get more relaxation next time."

42

Joe is becoming too routine oriented, even for his own tastes, every day seems to be the same as the last. He is such a fixture at The Goal Crease that it concerns him, and lord knows he doesn't like how his adventures and antics are well known to all the others at the place. He does like to keep things private for the most part unless they help him score occasionally with the unsuspecting ladies not familiar with his charms and quirks.

He is lying on his bed, drifting in and out, a beer sitting on his makeshift table, which is a cooler he brought with him, when he hears a light tap on his door.

"Hey, Joe, headed to the Goal Crease for your usual frivolous, unproductive dose of fake Florida reality and happy hour drafts?"

"I don't know, David, I think I need a new place. Saw a billboard over on 41 for a cool little place called 'The Office', looks cool, shows neatly dressed guys in suits sitting at a bar and enjoying adult beverages in a classy setting, kind of fits my personality and attitude lately. Besides, I think I am outgrowing the clientele at The Goal Crease, they aren't as sophisticated and stately as I am anymore."

"Yeah, that's definitely you, Mister Bud dollar draft Highbrow."

"It's getting stale at the Goal Crease, seems like it is the same thing every day, the same stories, same cast of characters, same drinks".

"Aren't you usually there alone during the days when everybody else is still working?"

"I need something different, I just feel this place, The Office, is that and I'd fit in there, you know?"

"Oh, it's definitely different, Joe and I have a feeling you'll fit in there really well."

"What makes you say that David, why do you think that? David shrugs and looks at Joe quizzically.

Joe rambles on thinking about a guy he sees often there. "Well, there is that guy 'One Eyed Jack' that lost his eye at a card game and he doesn't work, no place to go, just sits around the Goal Crease telling everyone he had the better hand, that's why they call him One Eyed Jack."

"If I hear that story one more time, Joe, I'll pull my hair out."

Joe looks at bald headed David shaking his head in disbelief. "It's just that I hear they welcome all types and persuasions at The Office, Joe, no judgement against anyone there."

"Oh, you mean, like, they allow Mexicans there?"

"Yeah, something like that, Joe."

"You doing anything later, David, want to go with me maybe?"

"You, the King of the Court at the Goal Crease request my presence at one of your drinking establishments? I guess the potato chip collection can wait, the only promising one someone sent was a Rachel Ray one from her fatter days, they are not so rare anymore. Besides, it should be interesting to see how you will react when we go there, should be fun."

"Cool, thanks, I'm even going to dress up in a suit like they wear on those billboards, so I will fit in, heaven knows I am a normal guy."

"Yeah, Joe, a normal guy that wears women's thongs and sings female parts at karaoke, what could possibly go wrong?"

"Just don't let anyone from The Goal Crease know, I don't want word to get out that I betrayed my buddies there, I wouldn't want them to think I am dissing them."

"I promise I won't Joe, they probably need a break from you too."

43

Joe and Todd are having their pre-Goal Crease beverage allotment as they are waiting for Joe to finish his phone call to his health insurance provider about his personal predicament. It seems as though one of the ladies he had been with recently remarked about the size of his manhood. Joe, being the egotistical, insecure guy he is, decides to take matters into his own hands, so to speak.

"Come on, Joe, happy hour will be over by the time we get there. I notice you've been on hold for like an hour. What gives, is someone giving free samples of Viagra or something? You never have the patience to wait on hold."

Joe holds up his fingers in a waiting motion. "Waiting to get through to my insurance company, Todd."

Todd polishes off his third beer. "Oh, ok, I remember one time you waited on hold for almost two hours for social security, and when they came on, you hung up on yourself, you punched a hole in the wall after. The only other time I saw holes in your wall is when those hot twins lived next door, you kept saying it was to make sure they weren't getting into trouble, that their hot single mom couldn't trust them at night while she was working the pole at Coochie-Ha Has, so you'd keep an eye on them."

"What can I say, Todd, I am a selfless caring fatherly type of guy that looks out for his hot neighbors' kids." Joe places his hand over the phone. "By the way, did you see my Minicam, Todd? I had to get proof of their shenanigans for their hot mom."

Just then, the canned music comes to an end. "Wait, I think someone is finally coming on. Yes, this Is Joe C., I had a quick question regarding my health insurance plan, does it cover an elective medical procedure I was interested in?"

The friendly patient woman on the other end of the line is trying to be courteous and helpful. "Oh, what procedure were you thinking of getting, sir?"

"Well, this is kind of embarrassing, but I'm thinking of getting a male enhancement procedure on my dick."

There is a deadening silence now on the call. "Excuse me, sir, on what, did you say?"

"My massive monster, my pussy pleaser, my wonderful wang."

The woman remains calm and tries to continue undeterred by this obviously ignorant phone caller and tries to remain professional and courteous. "Um' let me check to see if it includes that, what is your policy number, sir?"

"Ok, it's L as in Large cock, H as in Huge prick, B as in sweaty Big Balls, 1, 3, 7, X as in Extra Sized Dick, 2, 4,

6, V as in your Smelly Vagina, S as in I'm gonna Skull Fuck your mouth if you don't help me."

The woman retains her steady polite professionalism.

" Ok, I got it sir, that is L as in Pathetic Limp Dick Loser, H as in Hairless Small Dicked Homo, B as in Ball sucking homo, 1, 3, 7 , X as in extremely unbalanced, 2,4,6, V as in You'll Never get Vagina again you fucking idiot, S as in stupid shithead, T as in Tiny Transgendered useless dickhead."

Joe is not offended or put off by her return serve of vulgarity.

"No T at the end, thanks."

There is a silent pause for what seems an eternity. "It looks like you are qualified to have a prosthetic 2-inch extender inserted to make you a whopping 6 incher now. The copay is $599, but it is outpatient only and you will need to have someone drive you there, and change your bandages, and squeeze your member hourly for the first day to keep down swelling. It's probably the biggest you will ever be sir."

"Ok, thanks, my buddy Todd will help me, he's a great friend."

Todd overhears Joe's one-sided comment on the call. "Oh, hell no, I won't Joe, you're on your own, can't one of the bartenders down at The Goal Crease or Rick help?"

"Come on, Todd, Rick's running appointment to be tied up at the S & M club is usually at that time, and

Marissa has liposuction treatment for her ears the same day. I never met anyone who had ears like me. Come on man, I'd help you, or at least find you a toothless, needy old whore to help you."

Todd keeps creating excuses and reasons for not helping Joe with his unnecessary surgical procedure. "Can't your aunt's neighbor help you Joe? She could use a little extra bingo money, I'm sure."

"Come on, Todd, I'll even throw in a free round of $1 drafts at The Goal Crease."

Todd hesitates and ponders his own penniless predicament of no $1 Bud drafts at The Goal Crease this week. "You're lucky I didn't get paid this week, you owe me big time, Joe."

44

After the fiasco phone call, they decide to head to The Goal Crease finally. They arrive there later than they usually do and are a bit put off seeing that two complete strangers are sitting in their seats. Everybody at The Goal Crease knows that this is where Joe and Todd sit, what gives? Joe tells Todd that he has a solution to their quandary. Joe has this almost superhero like trait that allows him to pass wind on will, but not just the garden type wind, but extremely unflattering and downright offensive gaseous explosions, sometimes even registered on the Richter scale.

Joe walks up to the unsuspecting fellow beer guzzlers and pats them on their backs. Joe feels he is being civil and gives these fine upstanding gentlemen a chance to be courteous and remove themselves from his seat. The reaction to Joe's polite request does not go as planned when one of the guys tells Joe to fly away like a gnat or he will personally splat his tiny ass on the bar. Joe puts his arms up in surrender and turns around, acting as if to ignore the two guys. Suddenly, the one guy starts sniffing in the air and nudges his partner.

"What is that awful foul odor, was that you, Nicky?" He raises his head abruptly and detects it now too.

"What do you mean, Louie, I thought that was you. I told you; you shouldn't have had that cole slaw with your pulled pork sandwich." Louie knows it wasn't himself that made that smell.

"That is so disgusting, Nicky, you really need to get that checked or something."

Nick pokes Louie in the chest, and the two guys come to blows. The manager runs over and comes between them and asks them to remove themselves and take that horrid smell with them. The two slink off in complete denial.

The two seats open up and Joe gestures to Todd in victory. They happily settle into their preordained seats.

"Hey Joe, saw your pictures of you in your ahem, 'queer garb' posted all over the internet."

"What, where did you see those? Todd, oh no, how did that fucking David do that?"

"What are you talking about, Joe?"

"Well, Todd, I had problems on my computer, had a virus or something."

"Well, you do view an awful lot of porn sites, I could see how that would happen, Joe."

"Yeah, yeah but I never pay for it like you do, so I had the roommate look at the computer and fix it. He said, 'no problem, no charge'. I told him I had private things on there that I did not want to lose, and then after he worked on it, he claimed he lost my pictures and files."

"Did you at least back them up or download them somewhere?"

"No, and I really need them for my special dates on the net, damn."

"Joe, when will you learn you'll never find your perfect woman on there?"

45

Sometimes life imitates art and sometimes we oblit-erate any interpretation of it by our impulses and sudden actions. A little dose of sophistication and class can break up the monotony of days at The Goal Crease, Happy Hours at the beach, or karaoke at the local Moose chapter. Besides, the occasional attendance at a classy entertainment venue might be uplifting and educational.

"What are we doing at the Palm Beach Theatre, where is the ice rink or ball field Joe?"

"I thought it would not hurt to get some culture in for once, besides Romeo and Juliet is an all-time classic, Todd. I used to go to plays when I lived in New York City, nothing better for your entertainment dollar, you ask me."

Todd looks around at the place in a disappointed manner. "Are you sure you're not gay, Joe? Nothing beats ice hockey, the hits, the fights, now that is enter-tainment for your dollar."

"This play has an element of violence and risk; you should give it a try."

"Oh, you mean the productions where guys are singing as they pretend fight, that's real macho."

"Just enjoy it, who knows, you might end up liking it and wanting to go again."

"Doubtful, Joe, but at least they sell beer at intermission, I'm glad I snuck a few in for the first period."

The production begins and the curtain rises. The first lengthy act begins, and Joe settles in to watch. Todd is getting antsy about the first half of the first act and wants to leave but he sits and waits for Joe to make the first move and start to head out. Joe sits still and is seemingly very interested in the dialogue and action, even though it sounds like it is another language altogether. Finally, Todd can't take it any longer. "I feel a little out of place here, Joe, wearing my shorts and Rangers jersey, this does not seem like a Rangers game. When do they play the national anthem, I will take my cap off for it. Did they have popcorn at the refreshment stand? I need to go take a dump; this is boring."

Joe waits until Todd returns. He notices a subtle difference in Joe's attitude. "God, this is an awful production, Todd, sorry to drag you down here to witness this." He screams out so the audience can hear him clearly, "Hey, get a real job, buddy!"

"Joe, why are you yelling like that out loud, I don't think this play is supposed to have audience participation." Todd senses that the others in the crowded theatre are looking directly at them, some of them speaking in hushed tones and pointing their way.

"You suck!!!!"

"Joe, the people in the audience are staring at you, be quiet."

Joe yells louder. "This is a disgrace, Todd, we got gypped." Joe directs his unflattering comments to the stage," Learn how to act bozo, my kid's kindergarten class acted better!"

An usher rushes up to Joe with his little flashlight and directly points it in Joe's face. Some of the other patrons say, "Sir, you need to leave the theatre, you are out of control, and, on top of it you smell of rancid cheese and stale beer."

"No way, I paid money to see this piece of crap and I have a right to voice my displeasure, like booing at a hockey game."

All of a sudden, one of the actors pulls out of character and with his sword, he jumps off stage and whacks Joe in his mid-section. Joe buckles over in pain for a second to give the appearance of an injured hockey player during a game. Joe puts up his hands in a sign of defeat. "This is out of control, hey stop. I just wanted to show them how to act." He tries to change his tactics by getting out of his pretend crouch during the scene and starts flailing mindlessly as the whole cast and a few in the crowd pounce on him. Joe gets roughed up and gets black and blue eyes and his lip is puffed out noticeably, and he is physically thrown out the back door. The audience is now going wild and applauding, thinking it was actually a part of the staged production. Todd is waiting there with a beer in his hand, very pleased and smiling. "Only you can start a bench brawl at a play, Joe, good job old buddy."

"I can't stand bad acting. This was highway robbery, you ask me."

"I never saw fisticuffs at a play, this reminds me of those crazy soccer fans in Europe that start riots during the game. Thanks for bringing me along, Joe, this was fun."

46

Believe it or not, some nights in Florida get down-right frigid. Some of the places even have portable gas-powered heaters when the temperature dips under 60 degrees. Luckily, The Goal Crease is just one of those places.

"Mister, it's freezing in here, can you move the propane heater closer to me?"

Joe sees a damsel in distress and steps right up to be assistance. "Sure thing, sweetheart, I got it." Joe shakily handles the awkward heater, tipping it over and clipping the roof fan.

"Joe, what are you doing, it's tipping over, you're going to start a fire in here."

Joe clumsily tips the heater as he tries to move it. "What, I can handle it, Jeremy, oops, how did that happen?"

"You're dangerous, Joe, you know that, give me that before someone gets hurt." Jeremiah quickly swipes the heater out of Joe's hands and places it neatly near the lady.

"I'm just trying to help the little lady, what?"

"Starting the roof on fire is not helping, Joe."

"It isn't that bad, at least it's warming up in here."

The lady looks squarely at Joe only, ignoring Jeremiah. "Thank you, sir, for all your help."

"It was nothing, Miss, my name is Joe, yours?"

"There goes Joe taking credit for something he didn't do again" Jeremiah stomps off looking for his pool cue.

Joe turns his undivided attention to the attractive lady. "So, what's a gorgeous lady like you doing in here, don't you have a man or something?"

"He's a loser, no, I dumped his ass, and I am looking for a big, strong guy like you." She bats her eyes and Joe makes a gesture that she has something stuck in her eyes.

"My buddy Jeremy is a big, strong guy, what's wrong with him, he is the one that carried over the heater."

"I know, but I have a thing for short, balding out of shape middle aged guys, what can I say?" She bats her eyes again at Joe and gestures toward her empty glass sitting idly on the bar.

"Oh, well, I'm all that and then some, so what are you into?"

"Anything that doesn't hurt, well, too much."

Joe puts his left arm around the lady. "I like how this is going, nice."

She gets bold and blunt. "Do you have your own place, I'm kind of in between places."

Joe goes in for the kill, damn mating rituals and niceties, he thinks. "My van is in the parking lot and sleeps two comfortably."

She laughs and puts her hands on Joe's shoulder, as Joe tries to plant a kiss on her. "Slow down there big guy, I just don't go and get with someone, well, at least not in the first five minutes after meeting them. I need a few shots and a chaser; would you mind getting me that while I freshen up?" She gets up and heads to the restroom.

"Sure thing, Miss," as he watches her hips as she walks away.

Joe runs over to Jeremiah and asks him if she mentioned her name to him, Joe swears he knows her or saw her before. "Jeremiah, what did she say her name was again, I swear I have met her before."

"You seem to think you met a lot of other chicks before, Joe, you are always bombed in here."

"Well, this place does have a vibrant ambience what can I say?" Joe speaks in a distinctive accent and tone that doesn't sound like his own voice. "Hey, Alex, hook a brother up with a few fireball shots and a chaser for the little lady."

"Why are you talking like that, Joe?"

Joe blinks. "How do you mean, Jeremiah?"

"You sound like you are a gangster from the 30's or something."

"Here she comes again, why does she look so familiar?"

Todd pokes his head over from the other side of the bar. "She looks like that actress from that forgettable TV series "Perfect Strangers, Joe."

"It figures you would know something like that Todd, you must have been one lonely child, wasn't that Bronson Pinchot in it or something? I pleasured myself to some of the actresses on that show."

"Are you sure it wasn't to the guys on the show, Joe?"

"Ha, no, not my type, sorry."

She returns from the restroom and Joe clears a spot for her and shows her the drinks he got for her while she was away. "Hi again, sweetheart, sit down, I did not catch your name, here's your shots and chaser, bottoms up."

"It's Rebeca, with one C, I bet you never met someone like me with one C in her name."

"Nope, I can't say I have, you look so familiar, my buddy seems to think you were in a show in the 80's but I said you look too good to have wasted your time with that. I heard that guy Bronson Pinchot was a jerk."

Joe is taken aback when she responds that she was in fact that lady.

"He was very funny, actually, but that was long ago, and I am stuck here in loserland now."

"Eh, you get used to it, how long have you been down here now?"

"I was just in between jobs, it was supposed to be a temporary thing, been waiting for the right role since the series ended."

Joe tries to be helpful to the obviously needy actress. "There are regional theatres here, but I am not allowed in them since that incident at the Royal Palm Theatre."

Joe is pinching himself that he has a shot to nail a real-life celebrity. Won't mom and dad be proud of me now, he thinks. "So, you really that desperate to hook up with a loser like me, I mean, what, with you being a former star on TV and all?"

"Yeah, I like to see how the other half lives, sure, why not?"

Todd comes closer to hear what's going on. "Oh, Miss, trust me, he is the other half."

"Shut up, Todd, you don't know nothing."

The lady snaps back quickly, "what did he mean by that, why did he say that about you?"

Todd blurts out, "Because he is a freak and wears women 's panties and dates ugly chicks."

Rebeca holds her hands over her mouth to hide her reaction. "Oh really, Joe, you wear women's panties, that's kind of different and kinky, I never hooked up with a guy that wore those, what are you doing later?"

Todd is stunned by her admission, wait, Miss, don't you think that is kind of faggy and creepy?"

"It's Rebeca with one C, and no, I think it is kind of adventurous and daring, not like all the guys in Hollywood and on TV, now those are men's men, this is kind of sweet and endearing. Here's my number, lord knows I am going to be here awhile, seeing as there is no demand for a gorgeous slightly older 80s sitcom actress. Maybe I will start a reality show with Joe. Maybe we can turn your fetish into a reality show, if that freak Caitlyn or Bruce or whoever can do it, who knows, right?"

Todd tries to talk Rebeca out of her thinking. "Hey, that guy, girl or whatever has some talent, Joe works at a gas station booth and drinks beer every night, which doesn't sound interesting."

Joe tries to calm Todd down and change the subject so he can pursue his prey. "Todd, Todd, Todd, aren't the Rangers on tonight?"

"Oh yeah, I have to get back to my place and watch the game, they are playing the Coyotes later."

47

Joe is still dressed in his work apparel from his job as a gas station attendant. Usually, he brings a quick change of clothes before he enters the Goal Crease, but he knew if the others saw him in the outfit, they'd ask him if they could score gas cheap because it was one of those members only places where the already overly priced annual membership enabled these privileged special members to be entitled to a whopping savings of about 5 cents per gallon.

He spots Todd and waves to him. Joe is hiding his bandaged hand as Todd approaches him. "Joe, what is with the bandages around your left hand? Looks pretty nasty."

"Hurts like a mother. I need dollar drafts to decrease the pain. Keep 'em coming, Alex."

Todd notices Joe's hands wrapped up and figures he will appease Joe's need for attention. "I probably will really regret asking you, but what happened, Joe?"

"Well, I was at work, just hanging out, when a guy approached me at my booth I work at. He seemed a little shady, had beady eyes, so I asked him what's up?

He says, he has a gator in the back of his pickup, I'm thinking, it figures, another crazy redneck. So, I play along with him and go out to take a look. Sure enough, in the back of his truck, there is about a four-footer flipping and bouncing around like a Mexican jumping bean. I asked him where he got it and where he was going with it. He said he was asked to take it out of the pond in back behind your apartment complex and to relocate it. He asks if I would like a picture with it, that a lot of folks do that to send pics back home, so I thought, why not? Well, somehow, the gator gets free from the straps, hisses at us and snaps at me, then he jumps off the back of the truck and runs through the parking lot. He nipped me a bit, damn, gators have strong teeth. I think maybe he was trying to get back to his mommy."

Todd is unempathetic and shakes his head. "I think you have too much time on your hands at work, Joe".

48

As President Lyndon Johnson once said, "Sometimes you've got to go along to get along." Joe was never a big fan of boxing or ultimate fighting, much less a woman's event, but it was on TV at The Wing House, and he knew that the waitresses were hot there. So, Joe thought, why not go? He reluctantly enters the bar, looks around, bored, but notices a couple of the servers, so he changes his mind on the spot to stay. He sees the others in the back and walks up slowly. "Why did I let you talk me into coming up here, paying hard earned money to reserve a seat for a Pay per View event featuring women boxers, Todd?"

"First of all, Joe, the chicks are hot and what guy doesn't get turned on by seeing hot chicks sweat and kick the shit out of each other, besides, it's not like you paid. Our buddy Vegas covered your entrance fee, so quit your yapping."

"I still think it's a gyp anyway, and what's this, beers are like five bucks, that's gouging, you ask me?"

"Yeah, Joe, but wait till you see the servers, you will not complain, trust me."

"I still say it isn't real fighting, so ok, answer me this, let's say we paid all this money, overpaid for our drinks and food, we get settled in, fight lasts one round, do we get refund?"

"Yeah, Joe, like when you get refunds for getting kicked out of all the other places when you start shit?"

"That's different, Todd, that is called entertainment at your own risk."

"You are unbelievable, Joe, just enjoy the moment. Hey, Vegas, Rick, I got Joe to finally cave and agree to come along."

"Oh goodie, Todd, we were just saying we needed some excitement."

Joe takes a seat reluctantly. "Thanks for taking care of my entrance fee, Vegas, even though I don't think it's worth it."

"It's cool, Joe, besides, I am doing the manager and she let me come in free, kind of like later, when I get to come in her for free, ho! So, even exchange you ask me."

"You always were quite the ladies' man. Vegas, didn't you even tell me you once were Cher's boytoy?"

"Yeah, want to see a picture of her sitting on my face?"

Before Joe has a chance to beg off seeing the picture, Vegas whips it out and puts it literally in Joe's face. "Um, no, uh, sure, why not?"

Joe is impressed even though he knows it could be anyone. "Wow, Vegas, I never realized how flexible she really was, impressive."

He looks to his right and sees a voluptuous, obviously non-sports fan sitting next to Rick." I see you brought one of your friends from Coochie Ha Has, Rick, is she a big fight fan too?"

"Hey, anyone will be a fan for enough dough so here I am, Joe."

"Shh, I think the main event is coming on, let's watch."

The procession and build up to the main event are almost an hour long and Joe is getting antsy, he can only leer at the waitresses for so long without getting noticed. Joe hates to admit it to himself, much less the others, but he is having a good time. Rick, Todd, and Vegas are engrossed in flirtation with the gorgeous server. Joe zones out and is just getting into the fight when the opening bell sounds. Finally, after much pomp and ceremony, the fight starts, and the two opponents come out of their corners. Within less than half a minute, the one throws a roundabout so hard and catches the other off guard, that she drops quickly to the mat and is counted out. She does not move, and medical personnel arrive immediately to tend to her, the crowd is unsure of what is happening.

"Is it over already, Todd, holy shit, man, what did I tell you? First round KO, the intro and pregame hype were longer, what a disgrace, I am glad I did not pay for that crap."

"Yeah, you got off cheap, Joe, as usual, what can I say?"

"Are we leaving already Vegas?"

"I have a date, Joe. I don't know about you, but you can stay a bit longer, I guess, I paid for the extra package."

It looks like the entire place is emptying out already. Even though the fight was short lived, Joe wants to stay and take up Vegas on his offer.

"Where are the people going, Rick? Looks like a lot of good food being left on the tables, look at that batch of wings, what a waste, I think I'll nibble on a few." Joe walks over picking through the wings, tossing the drums aside. Just then, a group of 20-somethings comes from the front door and sits down at the open table.

"Um, sir, what are you doing, those are our wings!"

Joe drops the wings immediately as if he was caught. "Oh, I thought you left, I saw you get up and leave."

The guy is obviously aggravated and disgusted. "Yeah, to have a smoke, there is no smoking allowed in here, what the fuck, we didn't say you could eat our wings."

"Oh, sorry, but treats you right for leaving wings unattended in a place like this, geesh, like it's my fault."

The guy aggressively moves forward towards Joe. Rick sees trouble brewing, damn that Joe, he thinks, can't he even act normal in here? The guy starts to raise his fists to take a swing at Joe when Rick intervenes. Joe throws his hands up in a defeated manner, withdraws himself from the scene, and ducks into the bathroom.

"OK, ok, I got it for my buddy, Joe." Rick throws several large bills on the table.

Just then, Joe interjects, "Damn right you do, Rick, this wouldn't have happened had you guys not invited me here."

As had happened more than a few times since Joe was here in Florida, a security guy came up to him. "Sir, we have to ask you leave for breaking health laws and handling other people's food without their permission."

Todd is disgusted and embarrassed by his friend's actions. "Good job, Joe, way to ruin another fun night."

49

It's been unusually quiet the last few days, but David didn't mind. He could catch up on his potato chip collection in peace and quiet and not have to be dragged into Joe's drama, especially the mindless, endless accounts and completely senseless vignettes Joe would relay to him. He admittedly had a stable if somewhat boring existence, his outings usually involving the occasional trip to the doctors, but mostly a trip to his garage to putter around. David used to proudly say how he loved living in Florida, but Joe would call him out on that fact asking him where he had gone and explored that day? That was not the way to explore all that Florida had to offer here in the garage, Joe thought. All David could think about Joe was that he was a twerp.

"Hey, Joe, where have you been the last few days, I checked the arrest records, thought you were locked up again."

"Thanks for the vote of confidence, doofus, I was with someone the last few days."

"Oh, what was his name this time?"

"A chick, David, see, this is a picture of her." Joe is visibly aggravated. He is tired of having to prove his masculinity to the others. If they only knew how much zip-a-dee do-dah-zippee-dee-day Joe has had, they'd be jealous. Then again, Joe's standards weren't always on par with the other average Joes, was it now?

"Looks like a stock photo of anyone, woof woof, have your standards lowered even more substantially than before, Joe?"

"Hey, I liked her personality, besides, she let me do pretty much anything I wanted to do to her, she was putty in my hands when she saw what I was wearing under my pants." Joe parts the front of his hair with a devilish smile on his face.

"Are you sure you're not gay, Joe?" Dave gets up hurriedly."

"Hey, where are you going, David?"

"To the toilet, after that visual in my head, I'm going to blow chunks, thanks a lot."

Joe waits about 10 minutes, he hears David in the bathroom very loudly expelling chunks of pizza, pizza from Joe's leftovers that he left for himself for a snack later. Good for him, Joe thinks, serves him right for doing that.

David returns looking a little pale and drained.

"So anyway, what's new and exciting, David?"

"Got some interesting chips in, a very rare Gorbachev one and an even rarer Busty Morganna, remember her, check out this side profile, some hooters on that one. I will be spanking the monkey to that one later unless I get the munchies and eat her."

Joe suddenly gets up, pointing to his mouth and heading swiftly to the bathroom.

"Hey, Joe, now where are you going?

"Same as you, I think I'm going to be sick after hearing that."

50

Holidays on the beach in Florida are vastly different than the ones Joe was used to up North. The dress code is much more relaxed and casual, and the routines are vastly different too, how couldn't they be with it pushing almost 80. Whenever Joe used to attend such formal family functions, he played a role of sorts, whether it was as a son, a brother or a nephew, a grandson and later a parent or even an uncle. The advantage of being here this Thanksgiving was that you came as yourself.

Joe took it upon himself to rent a private room and have it specially catered, a kind of thank you to the guys for a memorable year. "Nothing beats Thanksgiving on the beach, guys. Beats being in the cold, right?"

Joe was appropriately dressed for this festive occasion. He wore his usual floral patterned swim trunks and striped shirt. He looks over at Todd and makes an observation on his attire. "Well, it doesn't beat your pilgrim outfit with the Rangers jersey and hockey helmet instead of the lame pilgrim hat most wear."

They see Jeremiah arriving in a pseudo-Indian garb outfit, the breechcloth. He was spilling well over the edges of it for everybody's tastes, but even went so far as to place fake wartime tattoos on his arms, and wore a feather designed war bonnet that looked so ridiculous the guys could not help but burst out laughing.

"What, you guys, none of you got into the true, genuine spirit of this sacred holiday like I did. I would have worn a pilgrim outfit, but I could not find the cool pilgrim hat, and large belt with the shiny buckle like the real pilgrims used to wear, screw you."

Not to be outdone, Rick arrived in his usual cowboy outfit complete with a cattleman hat, a checkered long sleeve shirt and Levi jeans, a nice pair of western style cowboy boots. For good measure, he tied a red and white bandana around his neck to make himself look classier.

They were sipping on their usual drinks when Todd thought to ask the others a poignant question. "So, ok, Joe, what are you most thankful for on this Thanksgiving?"

Joe knew what he would want to say, about the whole story of his arrival here, the constant feeling of being on the run, the fear that his fun could end on the flip of a coin but instead came up with an unexpected answer. "I am thankful for George Bush fixing, I mean, winning the election back in 2000, due to mostly what happened right down here in Florida."

The guys are taken aback, they never talked about politics ever, in all their time together here, and their association with each other did not even lend itself to talk like this, of any kind.

Jeremiah takes the lead. "Huh, Joe, why would his winning the election of 2000 cause you to be thankful, please explain?"

Joe, in his own warped way of trying to simplify and make sense of such a provocative statement starts to explain to the guys. "Well, Jeremy, because had he not won, the Columbia Shuttle would not have blown up, Hurricane Katrina would not have occurred, the tsunami down in Southeast Asia wouldn't have happened, and of course, the economic crash that caused people to use Chinese drywall in places like Cape Coral, therefore causing the chain of events to cause my calamities leading to my moving down here."

The silence in the room was unsettling. First of all, the guys were even amazed that Joe seemed to be aware of actual current events and recent history. Joe senses their surprise at his apparent knowledge of things other than the cost of his beers at the local taverns or the scores to the hockey games.

Jeremiah is at his wit's end and although he was no huge fan of the Bush administration, he had to defend him, at least. "What? That is crazy Joe, what about September 11, maybe the very defining moment of his entire presidency, how could you forget that?"

"I don't blame him for that tragic, horrible event in American history, I blame John Travolta."

Jeremiah slaps his forehead so hard, even the other guys jump. "John Travolta! How could you possibly blame John Travolta for the worst tragedy in American history?"

"Two words, did you ever see 'Battlefield Earth'?"

Jeremiah relents on his stance. There is silent murmuring between Rick and Todd. "I can see your point, Joe, that maybe was the worst movie of all time, I could see how that would cause terrorists to attack us."

To emphasize his point, Joe adds, "But to add to the list of what I do blame Bush for is that other horrible flick Gigi, with Ben Affleck. They all shake their heads in affirmation.

Joe turns his attention to the real reason they are all here, to have an obnoxiously large meal of meats, sides, desserts and all the extras and drinks galore. Joe was not exactly flush with cash these days, what with his part time gas station attendant job and none of the guys gave it much thought that they were trusting Joe to provide the bountiful booty based on those limited resources. They should have had their suspicions or doubts about Joe's kind gesture, for unbeknownst to them, Joe had done some digging on the internet and found a place that advertised a fully furnished Thanksgiving meal for a party of up to 20 at the very enticing cost of $5 per head, all the fixings provided and delivered door to door. Joe did not notice that the asterisked title of the ad listed the main entrée as "*Florida turkey*." Joe thought it must be homegrown or something on one of those illegal farms down by Sebring. Who cares, the price was right, and he could look like a big shot to his buddies and then they would be more apt to spring for rounds of beers at the bars they frequented.

The doorbell to the secret hidden room was rung and Joe found his way to the entrance, and saw a short, shirtless Mexican guy smoking a cigarette and holding a half used tin foil pan with a pile of food overflowing in the container. Joe was thrilled and happy to see such a huge portion and handed the delivery guy a Sequoia gold dollar as his tip. Joe thought he would appreciate it in honor of the holiday that celebrated the Indian and Pilgrims first Thanksgiving here in America. The guy goes to spit on the food, but Joe had taken it so fast and slammed the door, that the spit ended up on the grimy stained window.

Joe tells the guys to settle into their seats, they look around at the dusty plastic seats, no tables, and a step stool nearby. Joe goes to the makeshift kitchen that also served as the bathroom, uses a pair of tongs he found in one of the drawers and divvied up the portions to his now famished friends. He brings out each plate individually to them and tells them to wait so that he can say a prayer before they eat. His prayer turned out to be a children's rhyme, he remembered his aunt sharing with him when he was a toddler and had no relation to Thanksgiving whatsoever.

The guys are thoroughly enjoying this meal, they swear they have never tasted anything like it and kept asking Joe what it was, and why did it taste so yummy? Finally, Joe reads the small, printed title on the label attached to the tinfoil pan "*Florida turkey*."

Todd is the most technologically learned in the group. He never heard such a term and decided to google it. When he sees the description, he immediately throws his plate to the ground and grabs his throat and starts to make himself throw up. The others are frantic and ask Todd what was going on. He cannot talk because he is heaving gobs of the just consumed meal. Now Jeremiah and Rick are extremely worried, they have no idea of what is happening.

Todd is finally able to speak up and tells the guys that the turkey they were just enjoying and ranting about was squished turkey vultures, scraped off the country roads in central Florida, and served raw. The flavors of the other parts of the meal were derived from the excrement of the other animals they had consumed prior to their own demise.

Joe is oblivious and does not overhear Todd's babbling but sees Jeremiah and Rick pushing each other to get to the makeshift kitchen/ bathroom to purge their tummies of this squalid meal. A long excruciating hour passes by, and the guys get better where they can actually calm down, and Joe persists in his conviction to go through with the rest of the meal, and asks if any one of them wanted desert at least?

Jeremiah tries to stop Joe from telling them, but Joe blurts out what the label says, "it says Turtles or turtle pie or something, I think. Yum, that sounds good."

51

Joe and Rick are standing in Rick's house looking up at what used to be the ceiling, sunlight pouring in from the top of the structure. Rick looks around for nonexistent people, scratches his head. Luckily, the stripper he hired to paint the walls did an excellent job, much better than he could have done himself. But there was now the major issue of a gaping hole where his roof and ceiling had once been.

Joe tries to reassure him that things aren't as bad as they seem, but as is usually the case with Joe, his sense of decorum and the proper way to say things does not always come across the way they are intended. "Gee Rick, the place is coming along by the looks of it, but why can I see open sky here in your living room? Are you going for some sunroof effect or something?"

"Eh, the ceiling and roof caved in when we removed a couple of the beams, who would have guessed they were the main support beams holding up the structure? So now I'm going for that 'Newport mansion' look with the open space courtyards, get a little fresh air that way and feel outdoorsy."

Joe looks around at the uncovered walls, the hole in the ceiling, the barren floors. "What about the wild animals, won't they get in, and what about the crazy rains in summers here, won't the place get flooded?"

"Damn, that would explain the piles of fur I have been finding in the living room area. I thought it was just my mom doing quilt work and leaving small patches for a new bearskin rug."

"And what about the bugs, Rick? They get huge here and can be dangerous at times."

"I suppose I could put a netting on the roof to stop those. This place has taken more work than I expected, what was I thinking to buy a fixer upper here in God awful Cape Coral?"

"It's not so bad, Rick, at least you have a place to call your own."

Just then, a bird lands on Rick and poops on his shoulder, the bird turd dripping down the back of his shirt. "See that, Rick, I heard that when a bird shits on you, it's supposed to mean good luck, something good will happen soon."

"I hope so, Joe, because this is getting very aggravating and time consuming. I came down here to get away from my troubles up north, and this isn't helping. I thought I'd buy a small fixer upper and enjoy life at the beach every day."

Joe tries to calm him down. "That's why I own very little, buddy."

Rick looks over at Joe quizzically, expecting there to be a punch line.

"I may not own a nice place like this or have a showcase house to show others how successful I am or what I own, that it's better than what anyone else has, but I can say that I have many experiences and memories. Oh sure, not all of them end up good, as you know, but I never wanted to look back and wonder 'gee, what if,' understand? After all is said and done, what does having a million dollars in the bank and a sparkling place do for you?"

Rick briefly ponders what Joe has to offer but dismisses it. "Yeah, but Joe, you are like a nomad with no direction and no focus other than where you will be drinking Bud drafts every day. No thanks, not for me, or 99.99999 percent of the population. You are the exception to whatever rules there are in nature."

If Rick only knew the whole story, not just what he has seen these past months of Joe in Florida, how responsible he was, had kids, a house, all that stuff most others' lives are made of, of how Joe's destiny was determined by outside forces and influences, but Joe remained unfazed in making the best of his situation. "Suit yourself, Rick, but I choose to take advantage of everything this place has to offer and not be saddled down with an anchor like this, good luck to you."

52

Joe and Rick are having a few beers at a small park along the 41 where Fort Myers and Cape Coral converge. Even though it is illegal to openly consume alcoholic beverages in public, they are surrounded by a few groups of others doing it, notably a band of Puerto Ricans playing loud music and barbecuing on makeshift grills. They are enjoying the scenery along the river, abandoned and half sunken boats in the background. Rick has been meaning to raise his suspicions about Jeremiah, how he unexplainedly disappears for days on end and always seems to be around when mishaps occur, but Joe is in his usual self-denial mode consuming a few too many Buds.

Even though Joe is halfheartedly attempting to become a one-woman kind of guy, it is hard for him to change his ways. He has been showing an unusual interest in scholarly pursuits though, Rick thinks. "Joe, I noticed you have been going to the library a lot lately these days, what are you trying to do, get smart or something?"

"I am just trying to expand my horizons, learn a few things to be a more interesting fellow, you should try it yourself, Rick, old buddy."

"No thanks, Joe, I get enough education nightly at the strip clubs to last a lifetime."

"That must be an expensive lesson, Rick."

"Well, I did get a couple thank you cards from some of the girls for helping them complete their educational pursuits, although even the cards were spelled wrong, I would not say finishing GED courses is hardly considered higher learning. But let it be said I am not one to judge others, although I do judge them by the size of their booties and breasts."

Joe is silently flipping through a comic book he recently picked up at the local bodega. "Knowing you, Joe, I know there are other reasons that you have been obsessed going to the library."

"No, Rick, I volunteered to be a reader for the pre-school kids because that's just the type of selfless altruistic kind of guy I am. That and to check out the hot MILFS that bring the kids there. I thought it might be a good place to meet desperate single moms, it's easy pickings, they come to me, I don't have to go out and meet someone at a bar or club or anything. It's like shooting fish in a barrel."

Rick puts on a sly smile. "I knew there was a devious reason for your sudden interest in educational pursuits. You are like the wolf in the locked chicken coop, Joe, I don't know where you come up with some of your sick, demented ideas to meet chicks, but I have to tell you, it's kind of brilliant, honestly."

"Yeah, it is, I come across as some sensitive, giving, caring guy when I am reading to the kids, even though all I am thinking about is what their hot moms look like naked, it is win win, you ask me."

54

Jeremiah returned from a somewhat lengthy trip. He was dispatched to parts unknown to settle a turf war between gangs in Acapulco. He hated to bloody his hands this much, so to speak, but things had to be handled in a prompt and efficient manner.

In the meantime, Joe was doing his usual stuff and being the ass he was good at being. Believe it or not, it was more at Joe's urging than Jeremiah's that he needed this break, so when he heard Jeremiah was back, he contacted him. Joe had heard from a guy at the Goal Crease about the incredible fishing at the bridge over on Pine Island and though Joe was not an avid fisherman, he heard there were a few nearby places that were cool to frequent so he thought the guys would be open to the adventure.

Todd pulled out at the last minute to take care of a personal issue, a very rare case of something known as Jumping Frenchmen of Maine condition, otherwise known as hyperekplexia, involving an extreme reaction to stimuli that causes uncontrollable jumps and startle-induced falls. (Yes, it really exists, look it up on Google).

Jeremiah thought of bringing everything including his famous manmosas and a case of Buds for Joe. It took them awhile to get to the bridge after Joe made them stop by Marissa's to argue about who left what in the wash. Joe swore it wasn't his women's undies, that she must have met another guy that wore them. Rick told them he would meet them at the bridge.

They unloaded the car including the cooler where the live bait was kept. "I am glad you have all the stuff to fish, Jeremy, I haven't been fishing in a long time."

"No problem, Josh."

"Um it's Joe."

"Whatever."

"Not this again', thinks Jeremiah, for God's sake, he was only gone a couple weeks and Joe forgets his name already?

"So did you bring the beer, nothing like sitting on a bridge with a pole in the water and a case of cold ones in the cooler. I hope we don't catch too many fish; it will take up too much room in our cooler of beer."

"Not the way you drink them down, Joe, the cooler will be empty pretty fast."

Joe looks over and sees a glowing Rick wearing a fishing hat with a hook stuck in it, the hook rubbing uncomfortably along the front of his face, giving the illusion of a hook in Rick's eyes. Joe thinks the distracting item looks like a bad eye piercing those goth girl's wear. "Good of you to get out and relax, Rick, how's the place coming?"

"Not too good, Joe, I'm waiting for the permits to begin the actual work. I wonder why they're not here yet."

"Did you have to go to an office or something to apply?"

Rick grabs the bottom of his chin thoughtfully. "Huh, I thought they come automatically when you purchase the house, no wonders things are moving so slowly."

"I thought you went through this up north when you put up that other house," Joe asks?

"No, I just picked an open spot in a field and built it and there were no permits or complications. Everything is so damn regulated here, no wonder the housing market crashed!"

Jeremiah cuts off their discussion. Joe is opening the cooler to get his first beer of the morning. "Speaking of regulation, Joe."

"Yes, Jeremy?"

"You're a jerk, John."

"My name is Joe, why do you keep calling me by the wrong name?"

"Anyway, did you bring your fishing license?"

Joe is befuddled. "A fishing what, what do you need a license for, it's not like driving or something, not like you need skill to do this or anything. Rick's right, there are too many damn regulations down here. Why don't they put more effort into catching all the illegal

Mexicans down here instead of having rules for all of us law abiding citizens?"

Joe sees a small container with live shrimp. "So, what are these shrimps for, some munchies later?"

"They are to be used as bait."

"Whoa, wait, these things are alive, do they pinch or something when you grab them? I don't think they'll go on the hooks too easily. I am against the unnecessary killing of defenseless animals."

Rick pulls out a bottle of garlic and butter juice he has in his pocket, in anticipation of using it on his own personal catch later but has an idea to sprinkle the juice on the live shrimp, thinking the flavored shrimp will attract the hungry fish below. He douses the wiggling shrimp in it and heads off to find a spot to fish.

"Suit yourself, Joe, then you can just watch. There's plenty of fish in the sea for me then."

Joe finally succumbs to the torture of the defenseless shrimp. "Ok, but can you at least hook them for me? Sorry little shrimpy, the big mean man is going to stab you and put you down in the water to be eaten."

Joe casts his rod with no success. The hook, line and sinker keep getting tangled in the mangroves offshore. Joe is getting frustrated. "Why isn't my line going in the water, why does it keep ending up in the branches of those trees? This doesn't look like fishing to me, Jer. Can you help me get the hook out of the tree?"

Jeremiah throws his pole down, yanks the line and gets the hook out of the tree. Joe is thankful. "This should be easier now, thanks."

Joe accidentally snaps his reel in half and the shrimp goes flying midair and plunk in the water. He looks helplessly at the action unfolding before him, and pokes Jeremiah meekly on the back. "Jeremy, do shrimp fly, mine just went flying when I threw the line out. Can you put another shrimp on my hook?"

Jeremiah puts another shrimp on Joe's hook. If this keeps up, they will be out of shrimp very quickly. He sees an open spot along the bridge. "I think I will just drop it here off the bridge and see what happens, this looks like a good spot."

A few minutes later, Joe is yanking on his pole and can't get the line to rewind into his reel. "Uh, Jer, I think I am snagged on something, can you help get my line untangled?"

Jeremiah throws his pole down in complete disgust and wants to wring Joe's neck by now. "Why did I even bring you, I can't even fish because I keep having to do everything for you."

Joe gets defensive. "You were the one that said you wanted to go fishing. While you're here, can you do me another favor and put another shrimp on my hook?"

A few minutes later, Joe sits with his pole, the line going down to the water. He is bored and looks over at Rick, who seems to be having some difficulty himself. "How's it going over there, Rick?"

"Eh, ok, but I keep pulling in fish with only their heads on, strange looking fish here."

"Yeah, I'll say, but at least you are catching something."

"Yeah, they are biting, Joe."

There is a quick tug on Joe's line, but he gets freaked out and panics. "Oh, oh, I think I got something, Jer, can you help me pull it in?"

"Geesh, Joe, this is like taking my 50-year-old kid fishing, pull it up yourself."

"Ok, but it looks quite angry, man this is an ugly ass fish, doesn't look anything like what they serve you in the restaurant." Joe is struggling mightily and does everything wrong to land the fish. He finally is able to pull it out of the water, it is jangling on the hook on the end of his line.

"That's a flounder Joe, good stuff."

The flip flopping and nonstop movement scares Joe to the point that he won't hold the fish to remove it from the hook. "Can you take it off the hook, he doesn't look so happy." He notices that this little fish has razor sharp teeth in the front of its mouth. "What do you mean he has teeth, up where I am from, most fish only had lips, this is crazy. I think I am done." Joe is now beaming and proud of his conquest. "I expertly caught a very impressive, fighting fish. Take a picture so I can show everyone the huge fish I caught on my own."

Jeremiah is unimpressed but doesn't want to deflate Joe's excitement. "Yeah, that 6-inch flounder was a fighter."

"He fought me hard, Jer, but I reeled him in on my own, yep." Joe has a revelation at once. "Jeremiah, so, do you think fish sweat?"

Just then Joe hears a loud splash. "Jer, why did you jump in the water like that?"

"Because I can see them under the surface and since they're not coming to me, I am going after them."

Jeremiah breaks the surface of the water and holds a fish over his head.

"Good for you, hey what is that one you grabbed?"

"It's a snook, I think."

"Wow, she looks like a keeper."

Jeremiah pitches it away like a garbage bag into a dumpster. "Nope, Joe, out of season." SPLASH

"This fishing thing is very interesting; we'll have to try it again. Any more luck, Rick?"

Rick pulls up a half-eaten fish attached to the hook. "Just more heads, Joe, there must be some serious fish down there."

"Well, at least Jeremy and I caught a full one, I need a beer."

55

"How's it going, Joey Casanova?"

"I don't know, Todd, it's hard to meet the right chick down here, they all seem to have agendas or want stuff. How's your dating life going, Todd? I notice you haven't been around much lately."

"Well, it's offseason, so I have been getting out with a few regulars."

"Yeah, it is nice down here without the snowbirds around."

"No, I meant hockey season, thank God it only lasts a few months."

"Have you been seeing that mysterious woman?"

"Yeah, she keeps wanting to see me, but I always feel like she has to fit me into her availability, I mean, look, who wouldn't want a piece of this prime beef?" Todd makes a lame muscleman pose to prove his point.

"Yeah, you are becoming a lean, mean machine for sure. I never saw a guy bike around as much as you do and still be putting on weight."

"I keep telling you, it's my job, I sit around a lot, oh, and not enough sleep."

"Yeah, happy hours and eating at McDonald's three times a day have nothing to do with it, I'm sure. But yeah, I keep thinking about how I met Marissa and how we spent that horrendous night on the beach, but we did have a regular date after, I think it went well, she even mentioned meeting her mom after we finally did it the other night at her place."

"Whoa, Joe, that is a huge step for you, I am shocked. Some chick thinks enough of you to want to introduce you to their mom, that has to be scary to you?"

"I know, Todd, but there is just something about her, I can't put a finger on it."

"Yeah, she is, different, that's for sure."

Joe is distracted by a stunning redhead walking by and glances over at him. "Huh, what did you say, Todd?"

Todd is quick to notice Joe's reason for being preoccupied. "Nothing, just that the way you keep chasing tail, I can't see you settling down with one person."

Todd had shared previously of the seemingly secretive conditions for him to spend time with this supposed mystery woman, Joe is even having doubts as to whether she is merely a figment of Todd's imagination. "Look who's talking, at least I don't have to agree to meet someone only at selected times and locations when they want to meet you. I am a man and decide who to go out with and when."

Something is niggling at Todd about this woman, yet he wants to believe she is the real deal. "Just seems like she is holding something back, Joe. Women, who can figure them out, she reminds me of the 44-45 Rangers, lowest scoring team, worst goals against, Ab Demarco leading scorer with only 24 goals, like, there's nothing there, you know?"

"You don't have to tell me, my Sabres are there these days too, so what do you mean it's not there?"

"I don't know, it's just that she always seems to change how she is every time we meet, I like it, it's just unsettling."

56

Joe is sitting in front of the Lee County Jail, it is a warm and sunny day, the air is fresh, Joe breathes it in and is relaxed. Rick pulls up in his mother's 2002 Tan Buick Century, looking inconspicuous. He tries to unlock the automatic locks on the door, but they do not work, so he must reach over and unlock the door manually for Joe for Joe to get in the car.

"How did you end up in jail again, Joe? I swear I am going to change my phone number, so you don't keep calling me to bail you out of some stupid situation you got yourself into."

"But it's all your fault, Rick."

Rick is exasperated. "What, how is it my fault, Joe?"

"Well, remember you asked me to go to the Tax Collector to file for that permit for your cage catching contraption you use in your backyard?"

"Yeah, first of all, it is absolutely fucking ridiculous how many regulations they have here, how could you mess that up so badly that you end up in jail?"

"Well, I grabbed the pile of papers you said you left on the counter; I didn't know which ones you needed me to bring so I grabbed the pile on the left side."

"Yeah, the pile with the pink post it on it."

Joe is confused now. "Yeah, the one on the left side of the fridge, right?"

Rick slaps the side of his head. "Which pile did you say you grabbed, oh no, you dummkopf! You were supposed to take the other pile."

"Why, what was in the pile, Rick? It must have been pretty serious, the office locked down and a swarm of SWAT guys fucking attacked me."

Rick tries to calm Joe down. "Calm down, calm down, Joe, didn't you at least look what was in the stack of papers?" Rick realizes he left his other, let's just say, 'personal notations' of his overall feelings of governmental institutions here in Florida. "I was so pissed about all the bullshit regulations and permits and fees and fines and court appearances I had, let's just say I wrote a note of disapproval at the system, me bad."

Now he realizes his error in judgement and actually feels sorry for Joe. "How bad was it, Joe?"

"There was screaming and people ducking under tables and alarms going off, it was out of control, I froze myself, didn't know what to do."

"Did you at least pay the permit fee, Joe? I don't need another late fee."

Joe reaches into his pocket and tentatively hands the cash to Rick. "Yeah, why, did you need change or something? I still owe a tab at The Goal Crease from the other night, was hoping to cover it with the change left over."

57

Marissa was used to being secretive around her mom and family about who she was dating. She did not appreciate their opinions on men, nor have any similarities to them in regards of their tastes in guys. That changed slightly with this older man, Joe, who she had been seeing regularly and against her better judgement, succumbed to his incessant whining and pleading to be together She wanted to save herself for that special day but felt it was very special that he was her first. She was feeling she was ready to introduce her mom to him even though he was twice her age, ok, maybe a few more years than that even, but twice was good enough in describing him to her mom, she thought.

Sharon, Marissa's mom, was a very attractive, well put together lady, young looking, intelligent, open-minded, and loved her daughter very much. She wanted her to be happy with who she was with, unlike herself, who had a few failed relationships and never met 'the one'. She never wanted to be that mom that interfered in her daughter's business, but it was her daughter and a mother had to be motherly and guide her daughter or at least give good advice on matters of the heart. In this day and age of selfies, social media, and cell phones with cameras and the ubiquitous use of them, it struck her that she had not even seen a picture of this man, who her daughter was smitten with, maybe even strongly liked. Yes, he was older, closer to her age than to Marissa's and that alone could have caused an awkward situation of competition or jealousy among mom and daughter, but they had no common grounds of who they were attracted to. While Sharon went for the dark, handsome, rough around the edges type, Marissa was a little more open not to so much his looks, but that he has a sense of humor and just be himself around her. She knew of Joe's quirks and not only didn't mind them but admired him for his self-confidence. For the most part, Sharon was a good mom. Maybe this was a May-December romance on Marissa's part, and would peter out like most do, thought Sharon? Marissa had been on her own since graduating from high school and moved away shortly after graduation due to receiving a prestigious scholarship to Clown College in Sarasota. She could not adjust to the constant make up they had to wear during class, and eventually she quit and relocated to Fort Myers to "find herself." She picked up odd jobs and wound-up bartending at a place called The Goal Crease when she met this older, offbeat character. Sharon tried to be a good mom, but as with many of us, made some mistakes, lapses of error in judgement during her youth. One of those mistakes she had made about 23 years ago was about to inconceivably raise its ugly head today, of all days.

"My mom will be here soon, Joe, she was anxious to meet you. She was not thrilled I was dating an older guy but she's coming around a bit. Oh, that's my mom, Sharon, over here, mom."

Marissa waves to her mom, who comes up and gives a peck to her daughter. Joe steps away to get a few drinks for everybody. "Hi Marissa, how are you dear, where's the man you've been ranting and raving about?"

"He's over there getting a few dollar drafts; he was anxious to meet you. I hope you get along, he's a pretty cool guy, if not, quirky in some areas."

"What do you mean, Marissa?"

"Oh nothing, it's just that he has an unusual fetish for wearing women's panties when we had sex the other night. Sharon lets the comment pass unanswered and is shocked to hear that her daughter was so blunt and nonchalant about it.

"Oh, here he is, Joe, this is my mom, Sharon."

Just then, this older man carrying a few drinks for them walks up to greet her. Sharon is squinting and can't clearly see Joe as he approaches and finally comes into full focus.

"Joe? Oh no!"

To say Sharon was horrified and disgusted would be a massive understatement. Her mouth could not have dropped more in abject terror if she had seen the scariest vision ever, but this might qualify for it.

"Hi Sharon, nice to meet. I think the world of Marissa, and I know she is way younger, but she makes me feel great. By the way, you are very pretty, I can see where she gets her good looks, and she is quite athletic in the bedroom, if you know what I mean."

Sharon is suffocating and can barely speak, but she knows without a doubt who this guy was sitting in front of her, with her daughter of all things! "Oh my God, Joe, it's me, Sharon, from Puerto Vallarta."

"Who?" Joe is genuinely oblivious and unaware about who is standing in front of him and shows no signs of recognition for who Sharon is.

"You don't remember me, Puerto Vallarta, early 90s spring break?" Joe is trying his damnedest to recollect if he saw this woman before or not. There have been so many in his sordid past he has all but forgotten in addition to those he totally ignored. "Hmmm, you do look familiar, Sharon, Sharon, hmmm, oh wait, I remember now, we had a freaking unbelievable few days there, we must have done it like 20 times in every imaginable place, position, every second we could, cheap pina coladas too. I haven't seen you in like, what, 20 years?"

"More like 22 ½ years, oh my God, please don't tell me this is happening!"

Joe is perplexed and inquisitive and feigns acknowl- edgement of Sharon. "I never heard back from you, what happened?"

"Well, oh my God, Oh my God, oh my God!" Sharon is hyperventilating and feels like this is a horrible nightmare gone wrong and is about to pass out.

"What Sharon?"

"Yeah mom, can't you just be happy for me, for once? I am a big girl and can make my own decisions."

Just then her motherly instincts kick in. "Marissa, you can't be with him!"

"Why not mom, God you are so petty and vindictive, I finally meet someone who treats me like a princess."

Sharon cuts her off immediately and bluntly. "It's because you are one to him."

"What do you mean, mom?"

Sharon is now shaking frantically, almost in tears. "Marissa, meet your real father."

"What? No way, no way, oh my God, that is so gross, I can't believe it, mom. I can't believe you would stoop so low." Marissa is at her wit's end and still cannot believe this news.

Just then, Joe makes a quick quip to defuse the situation. "Well, I guess that gives new meaning to the term 'daddy' you screamed out the other night, Marissa."

"No, no, no, I can't believe it, I don't have daddy issues, I'm not like other girls."

Joe tries to focus on Sharon and what happened all those years ago. "So, Sharon, why didn't you tell me?"

"I don't know, I kind of hoped we would never run into each other again. You weren't really that good looking or that good anyway. By the way, do you still wear those cute bunny crotchless panties, you did kind of look cute in them, though."

"Those never fail me still to this day, thanks."

Marissa bawls, pulls strips of hair from the top of her head and literally sprints out of the bar screaming at the top of her lungs. "Mom, stop, I think I'm going to be sick, I've got to go, aaahhhhh!"

Joe misconstrues what happened and yells out to Marissa. "Wait, Marissa, were we still going to have that threesome with your mom like you talked about the other night?"

58

Jeremiah is still wrestling with how to get rid of Joe, but in the least messy and unviewed way possible. The syndicate is getting impatient and wants results immediately. The grand jury up in Buffalo is going to be called within the next few weeks but they cannot find Stephanie. Joe is out of town, whereabouts unknown to the local authorities but they had a tip he was somewhere in Florida. Jeremiah knows exactly where Joe is this very moment, on a "borrowed" pontoon boat near the Gulf of Mexico in Southwest Florida.

Among Jeremiah's limited skill set was the ability to take things when others weren't noticing. Joe has his usual stupid face unaware of what life really is like. If only he knew, thought Jeremiah, but as much as Jeremiah knows what needs to be done, he can't help but think how this goofy, drifting unfocused guy seems to be having fun and enjoying his time here in Florida. Jeremiah has a compromise to end his part in this whole ordeal.

He plants two bags of prime cocaine, well, baking soda mixed with baby powder and just a small enough amount of coke for an unsuspecting naïve idiot to be arrested and put away for enough time to let things calm down. There have been many stories about fishermen pulling in what's known as 'grouper blocks', where these massive fish are stuffed with illicit drugs and run across the waters and are illegally imported here.

Jeremiah had a twist on the idea by planting the stuff he concocted in living fish and having one of the guys 'hook' one by supposedly random fishing. Admittedly, his plan had a few holes in it to pull it off seamlessly, but he hoped by the time things were figured out, he would be far away. Of course, Jeremiah does not even stop to consider that just an arrest alone will not prevent Joe from being subpoenaed up North, or that the syndicate will be satisfied with that result. However, if he played his cards right, he could make himself disappear too.

"Nothing like boating to relax, especially this time of year. Thank your buddies. Jeremy, that was cool that they let us go with them, you remembered the cases of beer, right?"

"No problem, Jackoff, I brought our poles in case we stop somewhere to swim with the fish."

"It's Joe, how many times do I have to remind you, man?"

Jeremiah brushes off Joe's comment, as usual.

"Yeah, I hear this part of the Sound has great fishing."

"Like you would even notice between beers, Joe."

Joe is impressed by Jeremiah's apparent knowledge of the tides here. "How do you know where to go, and how to not get stuck in low water?"

"It's cool, we used to boat back home where we're from, piece of cake, you just drive the boat where the water is deeper and then when the bottom of the boat hits ground, you turn suddenly and don't get stuck."

Joe spots buoys bobbing up and down in the water. "Oh, ok, sounds simple enough, I guess. What are those poles doing in the middle of the water?"

"They are like traffic signals to keep the flow of traffic going like on the roads, they are called buoys, Joe."

Joe sees another boat that appears to be in the same lane. "So, ok, why is that boat coming in our lane?"

"Oops, I thought red meant stop, sorry." Just at that moment, Jeremiah looks up and realizes he is in the wrong directional lane of traffic in the narrow part of this channel and suddenly yanks the steering wheel, the guys fall in the pontoon. The other boater is steamed and raises his fists in defiance and speeds away.

The guys pull themselves off the floor of the pontoon and look around. Joe is captain oblivious, as usual. "Well, that was interesting, way to cut before that guy just before he got to us, that was good driving, though that guy was waving at us."

Jeremiah regains his composure. "Yeah, people are pretty friendly out here on the water, it's like we are all part of a secret club or something, some kind of boating fraternity, I guess."

"You do look like a captain of a boat, you look like Skipper from Gilligan's Island, hey, I could be Gilligan. Todd can be Mister Howell, and Rick can be that nutty professor. He sort of looks like him, you ask me. We just need two hot chicks and an old bag, and we would have like a Gilligan's Island thing going on. Hopefully we don't get shipwrecked like they did, that would suck, especially if we ended up on an island where there is no beer."

Joe notices off on the horizon that the boat they just had the encounter with is returning at an awfully alarming rate, and it looks like another boat is with him. Jeremiah notices it is some kind of patrol boat, he doesn't need this unwanted attention yet, so he literally ducks into a marina to blend in with other boats, but Joe won't let it go. "I think that guy appreciated you making his boat rock like that. How fast does this thing go anyway, I think we need to get away from him, he seems like he wants to race or something."

They sit in the marina a bit until the coast is clear and Jeremiah heads back to where he thought they were, only to go in the wrong direction from Sanibel. "Where were we going anyways, how do you know where to go?"

"I heard there were some good fishing spots off Sanibel in the Sound, we can head over there and see how they're biting." Even Joe seems to think they are headed in the wrong direction. Todd is half in the bag and Rick has remained silent for the entire time, keeping his eyes focused on Jeremiah. Something is up, he thinks.

Joe points off in the distance. "I thought that was Sanibel over there, Jeremiah."

Jeremiah is aggravated now. "Damn, no, that is Marcos Island. I thought we were going north, not south, damn currents."

Joe attempts to lighten his mood. "I never saw it there, that's cool, let's just hang out down here. I am sure they have big fish here too."

The guys reluctantly drop their lines in the water and start fishing. Jeremiah figures a way to slip off the pontoon, swim along the side and attach his "loaded" grouper on one of the lines. Todd whoops in fascination and is thrilled to pull in such a whopper. Joe joins in the celebration, Jeremiah slips back up on the boat unnoticed by the others. "What a catch, we will have a feast for sure, guys."

A few minutes later, Jeremiah yawns and acts like he is bored and catches Joe's attention, his ploy has worked in his mind. The coast guard looking for them from earlier might play into this whole scene even better than he planned.

"Are you tired, Jeremiah, I can drive the boat if you want, I never did it before, but it can't be all that hard."

"No Joe, it's cool, besides, we don't need to end up in the Keys or something. I told my buddy we'd be back by the evening."

"Hey, Todd, you got the best catch of the day, nice grouper, should be some good eating."

Joe is hungry now and doesn't want to wait till they get back to eat that delicious looking fish, so he looks around for things to start a small fire capable of heating up this delicacy.

The guys upfront are enjoying the gorgeous day on the Gulf, when Rick starts sniffing something, it smells like gas maybe, hard to tell out here in the open water. "Guys, do you smell that?"

Rick looks back and yells loudly at Joe. "Joe, what are you doing?"

A few sparks crackle from the base of the small fire and catch a few items and start smoldering. And Joe notices that a small fire has now started on a cushion with clothing laying on it. "Starting a fire to cook our catch, uh oh, that can't be good."

"You're not supposed to start an open fire on a boat, moron."

"I just thought we'd get a head start before we got to shore; I did not realize seat cushions were flammable." Now the sparkling flame gains traction and a full out fire starts to grow, and everybody panics. Rick, Todd, and Jeremiah dive off the pontoon, leaving Joe alone on the pontoon. "Ah, everyone overboard...." Splash...... The guys are wading in the water. "Why did Joe stay on the boat, he'll catch on fire, what is he doing?"

"Looks like he sped up, maybe he thinks he can drive the boat fast enough to extinguish the fire?"

All of a sudden, a flood of blue lights appears on the horizon, and they are approaching breakneck speeds. All that the guys can do from the water is watch the action unfolding. "Where did those coast guard guys come from? It looks like they are chasing him."

"Sure, he's ok, and we're stuck wading in this water, who the hell knows what is in here with us?"

"Looks like Joe doesn't know how to steer, oh, that doesn't look good, he is heading directly for shore!"

The coast guard patrol boats speed by the guys who are helplessly wading in the water, unsuspecting prey of possible large sea going predators lurking below. The patrol boats are hot on his trail so to speak, and Joe steers his boat to shore and slams it and runs away from the pontoon.

Jeremiah, from his vantage point quips, "Oh, this ain't gonna end well for Joe."

They see the coast guard members frantically land their own boats and run and tackle Joe on the beach area and start pummeling him. Rick quips "Oh, that had to have hurt, looks like they are roughing him up. Glad I have my waterproof phone to call someone and pick us up. Todd, looks like we won't have another way back in now."

"Are you sure we should leave Joe there?" "

"He'll be alright, we will catch him at The Goal Crease sometime."

59

It is a few days after the disastrous pontoon incident. Joe was hospitalized for three days and was released from protective custody on his own recognizance. For whatever reason, despite Joe's now numerous brushes and outright incarceration by local law enforcement agencies, it has barely, if at all, registered a blip on the radar of those legal enforcers back in Buffalo. The syndicate still knew where he was. Through complete fortune of the legal gods or just pure, sheer unadulterated good luck, he had somehow skipped by untouched on those issues.

After a very brief investigation, the Coast Guard found the obviously planted grouper bricks on board and no proof that Joe masterminded the escapade, so they had to grudgingly let him go. The others on board, Jeremiah, Rick, and Todd expressed no knowledge the bags were even on the boat, though Rick was now starting to wonder about his supposed comrade.

The bountiful catch of grouper, red snapper, and pompano that the guys legitimately hauled in was donated to a local homeless shelter that merely had hot plate cookers so that the sumptuous filets of exotic fish pretty much were wasted. Todd was still fuming about it, and how, in his mind, Joe really screwed up a productive and otherwise pleasant trip into a complete fiasco.

Joe and Todd are ordering a round of $1 Bud drafts at The Goal Crease. "You are such a selfish, unforgiving ass, Joe, that grouper was the biggest one I ever caught. I was looking forward to a lot of good eating."

Joe is drowning his sorrows in his beer and apologizes, but he gets sarcastic. "Sorry, man, I wasn't thinking about boat safety precautions. How would I know you can't start open fires on sea going vessels?"

Todd looks over at him angrily now, Joe has never seen this side of his usually affable buddy. "You just don't get it, do you, Joe?"

Joe stares blankly back at Todd. "What am I supposed to get Todd?"

"Everything you do down here has ramifications; you don't see that. Oh sure, you think it is all fun and games, like everything is a hockey game or something, but sometimes when the game goes to overtime, bing, bang, bong, one wrong move or play and the puck is in the back of the net, game over, you lose. I don't know what brought you down here or why, but you have to respect things here, it's not all tiki bars, happy hours and $1 Bud drafts at The Goal Crease, there's more to life than that."

Joe is incredulous and stubbornly reluctant to hear what Todd is telling him. "There is, Todd, like what?"

Todd continues rambling. "Oh sure, the weather is incredible here all year round and I can see where some fall into that vacation state of mind, but some of us who live here year-round and put roots down here have to follow the rules too, you don't seem to do that, why don't you grow up?"

Joe thoughtfully ponders what Todd just shared with him.

Todd hopes Joe will take his tough love advice, but Joe is uncomfortable, still undeterred about his choice of actions and activities down here and just wanting to escape what he believed was a miserable existence until his move here with unfettered freedom he never experienced before. Joe absentmindedly shakes his head in agreement but is still unsure what he wants to do.

Todd softens his tone. "Geesh, Joe you could have been badly hurt or worse the other day. What were you thinking, trying to outrun the Coast Guard?"

"I swear Todd, I was not deliberately trying to do that, the throttle got stuck and I couldn't control the boat, I swore it had brakes. Besides, how was I supposed to know there were enough drugs to kill a Budweiser Clydesdale horse onboard? Where did they come from? Who put that there, as it is, I now have another court date to explain my obvious innocence yet again."

"Joe, you seem to get into more trouble than everyone I have ever met, combined. Between getting thrown out of almost every bar and establishment on the beach, the various serious traffic violations, not to mention your other mishaps, I still wonder about the robbery attempt and that incident at Caloosahatchee Park with those two girls. I have never seen anyone with so many legal woes as you have. I don't know how you can afford the fines and penalties."

"I swear, Todd, it's just been bad timing or being in the wrong spot, I never had one incident ever with a law enforcement department. I was a model citizen. Oh, other than that misunderstanding at the border between Buffalo and Canada, but I swear it wasn't there in my glove compartment before we got to customs."

"Maybe, that's part of it too, Joe. You're in the wrong place at the right time or is it vice versa? See, Joe, this is what I mean, even this whole Florida thing for you, how has that gone for you to this point? Has it been what you imagined it would be like? Are you living in paradise, as they like to say, or in the penalty box with the other goons? When we met at the Goal Crease, I readily admit, I thought you were a little goofy, light in the loafers, mentally unhinged, but I thought you were OK because you were a solid hockey fan."

"Oh, you should speak, Todd, this from a guy that keeps a discarded frozen pizza slice you said you saw Wayne Gretzky eat at that pizzeria about years ago, and a seat from the Montreal Forum after it was knocked down."

"Joe, sure, maybe I take the sport of hockey too seriously, live and die with my Rangers, and sometimes when they are good, the Blue Jackets. The thing is, if you see the game of life is like as a hockey game, there is a beginning a middle and an end, except those times when playoff games go to overtime, Bing karma bang, bong, one mistake or great play, puck is in the back of the net instantly, game over, end of story. You have been living in that overtime period where it could go either way in a flash, and you might not end up on the winning side, like you have been since you got here. Yeah, sure we've had our fun, doing a lot of stuff that many others never get to do, and we've certainly had our share of dollar Bud drafts at the Goal Crease some would say an overabundance, but it's time to lace up the skates karma put on your garter belt and change your game plan or I'm afraid your Florida dream is going to come to a crushing loss in overtime of Game 7, and then, from there? If you want to make this work here, I suggest you change your game plan and prepare to win, like my Rangers do every time they take the ice. You need a plan, Stan, as in aim for the Stanley Cup, not just mindlessly skate around the ice in circles with no result in mind."

"Nothing like a couple dollar drafts after that little fiasco on the boat with you and Jer the other day right, Todd?"

"Sure, whatever you say little buddy, if by little fiasco you mean having additional compounding legal problems and, oh, just for the shits and giggles of it, a $15,000 estimate for dental work."

Joe flashes his jagged teeth now. "What Todd, my crooked and cracked teeth are cool, they make me look tougher like someone you don't want to mess with, you know, like a goon in the NHL."

"Speaking of a mess, Joe, that's why I was hoping to catch up with you here, I had a feeling you'd be up here like you are every day."

"Go figure right, Todd isn't this the life? You can't beat this, sunny warm day, a dollar draft of my favorite suds, a game on TV. We certainly have had some unforgettable experiences since that meeting at the Goal Crease. OK, some I admittedly don't remember due to alcohol hazing interference. I think we've been to the beach close to 200 times, we have seen over 100 hockey games on TV. I think I have done almost everything there is to do that this area offers."

"Yeah, but at what cost Joe, and are you better off than when you first moved here?"

Joe is undeterred and bull headed still "I think life is about having experiences, Todd, and no amount of money can replace those, right? Oh sure, I have gotten myself into a few, ahem, jams and even made a few good impressions on some, I think. At least those chicks that got to have that Joey experience, God, I miss Tung Hung Low, he knew how to have a good time."

"Yeah, Joe, but where is this all leading to, where are we going to end up down the road?"

"Huh, I don't know, what did you say? I was noticing that chick at the end of the bar playing with her hair, that's Joey's sign to pounce on another unsuspecting victim, or benefit of the 'Joey experience'."

"Can't you get serious, Joe, for once? Trying to help you out, pal, you're out of control. Don't you think a 50 something, balding, unsuccessful, drunken, unfocused guy like you needs to straighten out?"

"Why Todd?"

"Why, Joe? How incredulous, why? You can't keep going this way. One of us or both of us are eventually going to end up in jail, or worse."

Joe shakes his head in defiance. "Stop taking things so seriously, Todd we all take things too seriously nowadays and where does it get us, in an early grave unfulfilled, unpromised. Now, I am going to go talk to this young hottie and see where it goes, or we can sit here and mutually jerk each other around, and no I did not mean to say 'jerk each other off' although, I am sure you think that's what I meant. You got to stop taking things so seriously and lighten up, man. We only get one shot at all of this, and I know I have wasted too much time and effort trying to please everyone else. It's me time, pal."

60

We all have our own sense of religion and here on the beach, it takes on some unusual Sunday morning rituals not usually found in the confines of walls and steeples. Rick kept bugging Joe to join him on early Sunday mornings down at the beach, that it would be a life changing experience. As much as Joe loved the beach and having new experiences, early Sunday mornings were not the time to be upright, but he got up very early and drove down to the beach to meet Rick and see what this life-changing experience was all about.

He arrives there, and notices there are very few cars around. Rick told him about the little place near the monstrous resort that everybody frequented. Joe never liked going to that place, it was always jammed, other than the rooftop dining place overlooking the beach where Joe could sit on a swing seat and see the bathing beauties from high above.

Joe pulls up to the place Rick described and notices a huge line of motorcycles in front and to the side of the place. What the hell is this, Joe thinks, a biker convention, bike week, what? He somehow finds a tight spot for free. That makes Joe happy, but he is still wondering what's going on.

He sees Rick by the door and heads over to question him. "Why did I get up to go to the beach this fucking early on a Sunday, Rick?"

Rick is smiling like he has a secret. "First of all, Joe, I came here directly from Coochie Ha Has so it is not early to me, it's late actually. I have been meaning to show you how we and some down this way celebrate our religion, otherwise known as bowing to the porcelain gods."

Joe is not amused and sarcastically answers, "Oh, that sounds spiritual and wholesome."

Joe's curiosity gets to him, and he finally gets to the point. "What are all these Harleys doing here, and these guys wearing jean vests with patches and chaps?"

"It's a biker tradition here, Joe, come on, play along, you might learn something for once." Rick waves friendly to a gnarly, unshaven surly looking biker who staggers past to get to the altar, otherwise known as the bar.

Well, we are here and its noon somewhere, Joe thinks, might as well partake of things. Joe is starting to get into the spirit of the atmosphere. "Can we take a closer look at the bikes, Rick, I've never been on a cool bike like those, maybe get a picture of me on one, look at me."

Joe clumsily jumps directly on one of the bikes. Joe is straddling on one of the bikes and Rick gets alarmed knowing there is a code that 'you can touch a biker's wife, but never, ever touch his bike.' "Get off that, Joe, are you trying to get us killed?"

Joe gets off the bike and tosses his can of beer on the ground and is about to take a step when he stumbles and knocks against one of the bikes, causing a domino effect of the bikes to all go down on their sides within an instant. "Whoops" Joe says, as he heads to the bar.

The bikers all look around and see Rick standing by the now heap of bikes, his mouth agape. Just then, one of the bikers grabs Rick by his chest hair. Rick is pissed and swings at him and the two of them start wrestling, the others now forming a circle and watching the tugging match, most cheering on their fellow biker. No one has even started to pick up the bikes from the ground. Then an all-out brawl takes place, no one knowing what started this melee. This group of bikers are known to have fun in that manner.

Meanwhile, Joe is chatting with the cute bartender with tattoos as if nothing is going on. A bottle comes whistling through an open window and breaks on the wall, Joe does not even react to it.

Rick finally gets out of the riot and comes into the bar and takes a seat by Joe. They are alone in the bar; they can hear whooping and a few motorcycles revving up. Rick has a black and blue mark on his left eye and turns to Joe. "Nice day for church, huh, Joe?"

"Yeah, Rick, very spiritual."

61

Why is it that at national political nominating conventions, every state chairman pronounces that they are from the great state of wherever, and what they are famous for, or who their favorite son is. Just once it would be great to hear them say, "We're from the screwed-up state of Florida where all the miscreants, derelicts, illegals and criminals hiding their past like to dwell and ruin the place." It would be a more realistic portrayal, probably.

Todd and the guys came up with an idea to have an unforgettable pool party at Todd's complex. Todd found out that he could reserve it for a private function and as usual, Rick took off with the idea, suggesting that he spice things up by inviting the girls from Coochie Ha Has strip club to enliven the party. So what that he had to pay them their usual hourly rate and make arrangements to put up portable stripper poles poolside so they could make extra tips there? In addition, they would invite a couple bartenders from the Goal Crease to bartender at it, invite a bunch of the other regulars from The Goal Crease, and really have a blowout. They went so far as to walk around the pool and suggest how they could set it up. Of course, as they were doing this activity, adult beverages were present and some of the ideas went off the rails, even for the guys.

Rick had been at the club late the night before, and said he had to catch a few winks, so he found a lawn chair and promptly dozed off.

In the meantime, Joe and Todd continued their discussion of the party and grabbed a small cooler of beers and decided to sit out at the pool. As they were there, some of the younger female tenants of the complex came to get in their suntanning, laying out provocatively. Joe was leering at them as usual, trying to flirt with them.

Some time had passed, and Todd looked over at Rick and asked if they should wake him up. Joe looked over and said, "no, he looks peaceful, why bother him?"

Rick was wearing an orange shirt and it looked like he was getting more orange than the shirt, but Todd and Joe went back to flirting with the ladies by the pool. "Hey, Todd, I haven't seen Jeremiah in a while again, what's up with that?"

"I think the last time we saw him at The Goal Crease, he mentioned something about a mission to South America to save whales or something."

"That Jeremiah, he is a kindhearted good soul."

Todd tips his hand about what he thinks. "I don't know, Joe, maybe he isn't what he appears to be?"

"What do you mean, Todd, just because he travels often and can't tell us details of what he does, doesn't make him bad or anything."

"I'm just saying be careful Joe. He seems like a cool guy, and he does a lot of fun things with us, but do you even know where he lives? Have you ever been invited to his place?"

Joe is distracted by a utility worker who is nearby at the building adjacent to the pool. He is using one of the buckets to go high up among the trees and wires, but instead of using a tool or something, Joe notices him using his cell phone to aim at the open window. Just then he hears a shrill scream, the guy jerks and falls out of the bucket, thumps on the ground, gets up, jumps in his truck, and drives away in a hurry, the bucket still up, knocking some wires down. Joe doesn't say a word, just watches the scene unfold minding his own business.

Todd notices Joe's preoccupation and nudges him to continue their chat. "I am not sure he was in town or not when you had that memorable meeting with that blonde over in the park that tried to jack you, but you said something that night, remember?"

Joe barely remembers the night before but plays along. "Oh yeah, what happened again?"

Todd reminds Joe what happened but gets to the point that he wants to get across to Joe. "You said that the chick said something about owing a favor, and that has stuck in my craw since you told me. Hear me out, Joe, what if that was Jeremiah that set you up?"

Joe is certain that it did not happen. He is thinking of all the fun things he did with Jeremiah, golfing, boating, Pirate ship and on and on. As soon as he recalls all the times too, though, it is hard to deny that Jeremiah was the common thread, rather the one that was there most of the times these near misses had occurred. Joe being the way he is, though, chalked it up to coincidence and gave his buddy the benefit of the doubt.

Just then, Rick awakens from his deep slumber. He yawns and stretches and gets up and walks to where Joe and Todd are sitting in a shaded spot near the pool enjoying a cold beverage. He is bright red, the color of his skin clashing with the bright orange shirt he was wearing. Joe looks up cheerily. Hey, Rick, you're looking a little burnt there, buddy."

"Why did you let me sleep so much, what time is it?"

Joe looks at a clock by the pool and tells him the time. "You looked like you needed to sleep, we didn't want to bother you, besides, you kind of look good in that bright orange shirt, you can't tell where it ends and your tan shows. By the way, what are those bumps on you, yikes."

Rick looks down and scratches frantically. "Ouch, I think I've been stung or something, didn't you guys notice anything while I was asleep?"

The only thing the guys noticed were the scantily clad women, but no, they said, they did not notice him swiping or anything. "Don't worry about it, Rick, we will get you a beer, it will feel better eventually."

62

Growing up near the Canadian border, ice rinks were plentiful, especially outdoor ones, some up to almost six months per year. Joe played a little hockey as a kid and was actually pretty speedy and could skate around the others. Things changed quickly. When he was about 15 years old a 190-pound player nailed him along the boards, and was just as fast as him, Joe knew he could not keep playing.

Here in Florida where anyone could be what they want to be, he could reinvent himself. Todd had heard that there was an unpublicized pick-up game of hockey among the previous legends of the game at the local ice rink. He somehow found out about it, got in touch with one of the greats and convinced him to let his buddies and him play a pickup game against them. Even though many of them had been retired for as long as how old Joe was, they still were pretty good, but Joe wanted to show them he could stay up with them.

"A pickup ice hockey game against some of the legends of the game in July, how cool is that Todd?"

"Yeah, Joe, I heard some of the old timers get together once in a while to relive their past glories, but man, it seems too hot though."

"Aw, Todd, come on, I bet most of the current Rangers skate all year round, I just hope we brought enough beer to hydrate between shifts."

Joe looks around the makeshift locker room the rink allowed them to use. It was the open space under the stands, the rink was generous enough to place a couple of benches near the back wall. Joe looks around and sees that no one is matching like a real hockey team does. Jeremiah's entire experience in goal, if you even want to call it that, was a stint with the girls' field hockey team when he had to fill in when one of the girls got a case of hoof and mouth disease before the game. "Hey Jer, I like your Freddy Krueger goalie mask, rubber boots instead of skates and that Swat team shield as a chest protector. They are going to have a tough time slipping a puck between the pipes on you. Your field lacrosse prowess as a goalie will definitely come in handy, I'm sure."

Jeremiah realizes he is in over his head but was interested to see if any of the old timers were former Philadelphia greats of the past, from their Stanley Cup era. "I look stupid, Joe, I never played ice hockey before."

"You'll be fine, Rick over there will defend most of the shots."

Rick is sitting on the bench bare chested with suspenders running along his chest, his now protruding belly hanging over his extremely tight hockey pants. "Yeah, Joe, I am glad I kept my CCM skates, Cooper shin guards, and Sherwood stick from when I played in the late 60's. Nobody will get around me, but I haven't played in years, these skates were the most popular brand then."

"Yeah, Rick, I can see how the plastic oversized boots were all the rage."

"Joe, did you forget to bring your extra small size cup to protect your private parts? Not that you need protection there from what I hear."

Joe misplaced his gear years ago but had one fond relic from his youth that he kept. He cut out foam pads from a couch left on the side of the road and tied a ribbon around them to use as shin guards, then used his bike helmet and taped a wire mesh metal screen around the front of it and taped it along the sides. "I sure, did, Rick, and even wore my old Sabres jacket though it is kind of making me hotter in the 90 degrees plus heat."

The anticipation of skating with some of the most famous players of all time thrilled Joe. He could show everybody how athletic he still was after all these years. The game was only supposed to last about an hour, and most of the team had not been on the ice in years so they rented ice time before the actual game to get a little rust out.

The old timers, the former NHL players were already on the ice, shooting around and catching up with each other. Joe thought he'd get a little peek at the competition when Todd notices Joe on the other side of the ice with the NHLers. "Hey, Joe, why are you taking warmups and shooting at the other goalie, you're supposed to be on our side of the ice".

"Whoops, Todd, I had hoped that was our team, besides, I want to check out any weaknesses their goalie might have."

"That's Rogie Vachon, he's like 75 now, probably can't get on his feet so quickly anymore, we should be able to score a bunch on him."

Joe is feeling confident, maybe even downright cocky. Todd looks up at the ice and sees a familiar face to him and Joe. "Don't look now, Joe, it's Kris Draper, remember we saw him at the Goal Crease that one night?"

"Yeah, Todd, that is definitely him, I am going to go up and tell him that was him at The Goal Crease that night, that bastard."

Joe skates over and has trouble stopping properly, the ice chips coming up on the player's shin guard.

"Hey, Kris, remember me from The Goal Crease?" The player doesn't back off. "No, I don't, Joe from Buffalo, why don't you go back to The Goal Crease, you slovenly drunk bastard, before I knock that stupid shit eating grin off your face."

Joe is pouting like a little kid. "See, Todd, I knew that was him, hey Kris, watch your back, man, I will be coming for you."

"Oh, I am sure he is terrified of a 5'5 inch, 170 pounds, 50 plus year old drunken stupor non athlete on skates for the first time in over 20 years, Joe."

"The guy is so full of himself, mister big man at The Goal Crease, 'oh, look at me, I am Stanley cup winning Kris Draper,' he needs to be knocked down a peg from his perch. Besides, my motto is 'the bigger they are, the harder they fall'."

The periods of play were to be 15 minutes nonstop time, in other words, just a straight 15 minutes running time, no stoppages of play. The first period was disastrous and without even trying, the former NHL players put 14 goals on the board. Joe was not disheartened by their effort and thought he himself played ok. The former players were lucky, he thought.

They go to the bench to change sides, have a small break. The guys get beer out of the cooler, one of them even lights a cigarette on the bench. "Come on, guys, we only gave up 14 goals in the first period, it ain't so bad at least Jeremiah made that save on the dump in by Carol Vadnais."

"Yeah, Joe, he was never much of a scoring defenseman from what I remember."

"I never realized how fast some of these guys still are, pretty good for 70+, and your boy Kris Draper dropped back to defense after he scored 5 goals, what a guy."

"Yeah Rick, I meant to ask you if you get a chance and we ever get possession of the puck to drop one in Kris' corner, I am going to show him how to properly forecheck. He has been antagonizing me the whole game and let's just say it's time to make reparations for it."

"Ok, Joe, if you say so."

The action, or rather the one-sided direction of play continues in the second period and the barrage of goals keeps coming. Joe's team does not even get one shot on the goalie.

Later in the period, Rick finally gets an opening and flips the puck into the defensive corner on Draper's side. Joe sees where the puck is rolling and gets a sudden burst of energy.

Todd and Rick take a look at Joe, who is picking up speed to race to the corner. "What is Joe doing, did he just take a flying leap and try to sumo kick Draper down? "

The two verbally comment on the sad action taking place in the other end's corner. "Yikes, he looks like a cat in heat flipping out in midair, it looks like Draper brushed him off like a gnat."

Joe gets himself up off the ice surface, glares over at Kris Draper and starts yelling at him and drops his gloves as if to imitate a hockey fighter.

"Now what's he doing, he is chirping at Draper now, uh oh, he just dropped his gloves, that might not go well."

"Should we jump in for Joe's sake?"

Rick slows Todd down from trying to jump into the fray. "Nah let him discover the violence and power of a professional hockey player's bare hands on his noggin, I am sure he won't forget it."

The 'fight' is over as fast as it began. Kris Draper hits Joe squarely in the jaw, Joe drops like a bag of pucks.

"Holy shit, he dropped Joe in one punch, I never realized just how fast these guys' hands are in hand-to-hand combat, wow."

Joe is motionless and isn't getting up anytime soon.

"Looks like Joe is out cold, what should we do, Rick?"

Rick pulls up his sleeve and checks his watch." We only have ice time for 2 hours, why waste time cleaning him up, let's just play around him, he will be ok, he looks peaceful, maybe the Zamboni will wake him up after?"

63

Every once in a while, Joe and his buddies like to be mentally challenged by mysteries. Joe saw a billboard outside of The Goal Crease and decided to pester the guys to go on the Mystery train ride and solve the mystery. To get their full support and participation, Joe even agreed to get a couple of rounds of beers at The Goal Crease, but only if they were domestic drafts.

Joe, Todd, and Jeremiah arrive early at the train and head towards the back of the train in hopes of finding the bar car.

"This is cool we are doing the mystery train ride, Joe, I can use it as a setting for a book I'm writing."

"You write too, Jeremy? I didn't know that. It seems like you are always travelling."

"You're such an ass, Jim, I hope everything you love dies in your arms."

"Whoa, such hostility, man, what gives?"

"Well, I write in between jobs, I mean sales, it gets stressful at times making my quotas."

"Well, as long as you don't write me up as the villain in it."

"Trust me, Joe you're not smart enough to be one of those, no worries."

"Well, anyway, I hope they have a bar car on this thing, my extraordinary powers of deduction are always heightened when I am inebriated."

"When are you never that way, Joe?"

"When I'm sleeping? I keep trying to get my physician to give me an IV feeder for beer while I'm sleeping, but she does not see any health benefits to it. Some people take their jobs too seriously. I did get her to get me a sample one and I tried it a few nights, but I kept pissing my bed, I did not think that through, I'm afraid."

They look around at the others, sizing up the competition and guess who could outwit them.

Jeremiah is eager to prove his masterful powers of deduction. "So do you know what the mystery involves, Joe?"

"No, I guess we have to keep our eyes open for clues."

Joe spots a handsome woman looking around sheepishly, and nudges Jeremiah. "Look at that lady over there with the stupid hat, I bet she is a part of this."

Joe is inquisitive about this lady who appears to be out of place at this event "Miss, I noticed that stupid hat, does that mean you're involved in this mystery?"

The woman is offended at the stupid question this odd man proposed. "No, idiot, it's my grandmother's boutonniere, it's a precious heirloom and I like wearing it."

It looks like a pimp's feather hat he once saw from Baretta reruns. "Oh, it's very nice, I like the pimp feathers velcroed on the back of it."

The lady looks at Joe indignantly and moves on. Joe takes a deep whiff of the air as she passes by him. He smells a malodorous odor. "What's that smell, oh, that must have been me, that damn cheap draft beer they serve on here."

Todd briefly notices a suspicious man boarding the train. "How about that guy over there, Joe, he has beady eyes, I don't like the way he looks, he looks guilty of something, wait, isn't that Rick?"

"Yeah, I can tell by the cowboy outfit he is wearing, he really loves those boots, even on 90 plus degree days. I wonder what he's doing on here, I did not peg him as the scholarly sleuth type of guy."

"Yeah, the only thing he likes solving is what chick to have dance for him at Coochie Ha Has every night." Rick moves his hands quick as a magician, no one else but Joe spots the sudden movement.

"Hey, did you see that, Jer, it looks like he took something off that handsome woman I was just talking to."

Joe thinks to himself, 'no, he couldn't be the criminal in this mystery, it would be too obvious'.

The train leaves the station and soon afterwards, a loudspeaker comes on and the conductor speaks. "Attention ladies and gentlemen, it seems like we have discovered a body in the 2nd to last car before the caboose."

The crowds of people start to go to the back of the train to discover the first clue. Joe is lagging decisively behind the others.

"Speaking of cabooses Jeremiah, did you get a gander at that black chick's caboose, I'd love to run a mystery train on her. Maybe Rick's diversion was a part of this mystery?"

"Let's keep our mind clear to solve this mystery, Joe, I plan to take home the fake bronze plated gold medal for solving the mystery."

Joe and Jeremiah walk towards the back of the train, they finally get there after Joe stops at the bathroom. They look closely at the fake dead body, it looks faintly familiar to that chick, Rebeca with one C that Joe met at the Goal Crease that one night.

Joe and Jeremiah are no Sherlock Holmes and Watson, but they approach the staged scene.

"Look how the body is laid out, Jeremiah, who do you think did this?" Joe tried to sound knowledgeable about finding bodies.

Jeremiah kneels to look more closely at the staged body lying there and comes to an immediate conclusion. "It looks like the work of the 'Mad Maricon,' a slaying technique only found in the deepest parts of the Yucatan in Mexico. He is a mean son of a bitch if there ever was one, I've seen this work before."

Joe is perplexed and wonders how Jeremiah came to that quick synopsis. "Huh, what do you mean, how would you have seen this before?"

"Oh, I watch a lot of crime specials on the Oprah Winfrey channel. She has an unhealthy obsession with grisly foreign drug related gang murders I think."

Joe looks around at about the half dozen people within sight. "I don't see anyone that looks like a Mad Maricon on here, do you?"

"Legend has it he can change his appearance magically, Joe, he can even turn himself into a rooster."

Joe remembers his strange encounter with the woman before the train departed. "Wait, did you say rooster, do roosters have feathers Jeremiah?"

"Most roosters do although I know there are some featherless roosters used for cock fighting, why?"

Joe laughs hysterically out of control.

"Why are you laughing, Joe"?

"You said cock fighting, that is funny, ha ha. No, but that lady we just met had feathers attached to her stupid hat. Could it be? No, no way. I must be imagining things."

Jeremiah grabs Joe and shakes him almost violently. "No, Joe, you might not be on to something, she did have a longer neck than usual, the sort of neck you'd love to twist and hear cracking, not that I have ever heard that noise, personally, did she say anything unusual or make any funny noises when you talked to her?"

Joe does not recall any noises or sounds but makes an offhand comment. "Come to think of it she did have a foul odor, I thought it was me, but I did not remember blowing any wind."

Jeremiah becomes pensive and points his finger along his mouth. "How did he/she/it get back in the car and do the murder and then get back over here without anyone noticing? We have to figure that part out, but I think we are on to something Joe, I'm glad I deduced those clues."

Joe suddenly loses interest in this game of sleuthery. "Good work, Jer, I am overdue for a beer, do you need another one?"

"No, I'm good, I need to talk to that woman and find out if she was the one that did the murder so I can win the medal."

Jeremiah sneaks away and pulls up behind the woman and whispers to her. "Pulling the old rooster trick, are we, Maricon?"

"Ah, Jeremiah, we meet again, how did you figure out it was me?"

"My buddy mentioned velcroed feathers and a foul odor, besides the victim had a receipt from Taco Bell for the Chalupa Grande. What is it with you Mexican drug gang members and Taco Bell? By the way, you are a pretty homely lady and although I think my buddy Joe would go for a chick like you, you can't fool me."

"Ah, we have had our legendary confrontations over the years, amigo, but sorry to see them end so suddenly and pathetically, Sir Jeremiah."

"Have you sunk this low that you have to play a villain on a cheesy mystery train ride in Fort Myers, FL?"

"Times are a tough, my dear old friend, ever since that new gang, the Grumpy Grannies took over in the southern part of Mexico, business has dried up, we can't even control the kids' lemonade stands like we used to. They are ruthless, don't let the blue wigs and glasses around the chains on their neck and fake dentures fool you. So, are you going to turn me in and take home the bronze plated fake gold medal?"

"No, I haven't the heart to be so cruel and calculating, let me just push you off the train here before it stops, I'll just tell them you slipped away."

"Till we meet again, Jeremiah." Jeremiah whacks the villain over his head and violently pushes him off the platform before the caboose.

Unfortunately, the train was going over a steep embankment and the villain fell to his death.

After the crew lost track of the culprit's whereabouts, they decided to award the medal to Jeremiah for taking the mystery too seriously.

Joe congratulates Jeremiah "Good job figuring out who the villain was, Jeremiah, how were you able to deduce who the culprit was, there were so many beady eyed characters around. I never thought anyone would figure it out."

"Well, Joe, like I said, I was familiar with the handiwork, oh, that and the Taco Bell receipt left on the vic gave me a good idea of who it was. Know thy enemy, Joe, know thy enemy."

Joe suddenly remembers he saw Rick aboard and initially had his suspicions of him. "Where's Rick? I thought he had something to do with it."

Rick grabs the guys' attention by waving at them from the back of the railcar. "Here I am, Joe, I had nothing to do with it, why would you think I was involved?"

"Because I saw you take something from that handsome lady with the stupid hat. I thought you were part of the deception, what were you doing?"

Rick shrugs nonchalantly, placing his hands in his pockets. "Let's just say I spotted an opportunity to feed my nightly habit of attending the club. It was like plucking feathers off a chicken."

Joe is still not convinced." I thought it was a rooster."

64

Talk about surprises! Lots of times, we think we know our friends and family, but sometimes we are so involved in our own life that we barely pay attention to what's really going on with others, or sometimes we don't even care to know maybe? Call it self-absorption or complete callousness, but the fact is, most of us don't give a crap about what others are doing.

Joe received a fancy invitation to some hoity toity private club on Captiva Island for a very formal, fancy party, actually, a wedding! The Groom to be one was one Todd that he had hung around with over these past months. It was such a classy affair that Joe had to go and rent a tux for it. Was this some kind of joke? Was Todd playing a joke, or worse, was it one of those shotgun weddings that we often hear about, especially in the South?

Joe can dress up nicely when he has to, but the last time he was dressed this well was his own wedding many, many years ago. He takes an Uber over in anticipation of consuming many beverages this evening. That was the best thing about going to a wedding, Joe thought, one can drink as many beers as they can possibly handle. The Uber cost a bit more than he anticipated. No problem, he thought, he will deduct from his gift.

He arrives somewhat early and sees Todd who is shaking uncontrollably. "Well, Todd, I never thought I'd see the big day, you are finally marrying that woman you drove your bike to meet all those times, she seemed so mysterious, not letting you see where she lived. I always found that to be odd. Did you at least meet her folks before the wedding?"

"Well, turns out she is also a huge Rangers fan and wanted to see if I was as into them as much she is, and I told her I am for sure, even showed her the Wayne Gretzky pizza slice. Her folks are long gone, but I found out she inherited more money than you can imagine, Joe."

"Really, how much are we talking about?"

"Let's just say, you will never guess what her wedding gift is to me."

"Joe was thinking of something Todd would appreciate. "No, what, one of those cool electric bikes you were looking at when we went to Naples that one time?"

"Nope, this woman has enough to buy me a lot nicer things than that. You know how I usually met her over on Sanibel Island?"

"Yeah, you said you would ride your bike with her, and she would always be showing off her body to everyone."

"Well, she lives in South Shores over in Captiva, that exclusive area. Her dad founded Wausau Lumber Company and was worth billions. She is sole heiress, and get this, Joe, I swear I never knew she was that loaded, but on top of it, she proposed to me. When she told me how wealthy she was, I played hard to get, but she wanted her man, and she was obviously desperate to do anything to land him, ME, that is."

Joe is thoroughly blown away by this information. "I can't believe a loaded, gorgeous chick like that would go for a guy like you, no offense."

"Hey, I'm quite a catch for the right woman, if you ask me."

"Yes, you are, Todd, yes you are. So, you never told me what her wedding gift to you is?"

"Well, you know how I like the Rangers?"

Joe senses where there is going and cannot contain himself. "No way."

Todd blushes profusely. "Yes, way. We negotiated it like it was a trade and she finally agreed to buy them for me if I have Esa Tikkanen as my best man, so sorry for not asking you."

Joe is relieved he was not named best man, the expense of it a deterrent enough to him. "That sounds like a win-win for you, no worries."

"Well, she made me promise to not trade away the best player. She knows I am still pissed at him for agreeing to be traded to the Rangers. Oh, and she gets to screw the captain of the team once a month."

"So, wait, what does she get out of this deal?"

"ALL THIS" ....zip........Joe puts his hands up hastily in front of his eyes but the damage has been done already. "I did not need to see that, Todd, put that away before someone gets hurt."

"Besides, the wedding reception is going to be cool, all the 94 Rangers Cup Team is invited, oh, except for Jim Hiller. He is currently incarcerated for doing something naughty to mountain goats out West. Todd remembers another condition of agreeing to wed. the heiress "We also had to make a concession to the Rangers parent company, they insisted Bryan Adams perform at the reception, no charge to us, of course. I guess his schedule was open."

"I am so shocked by all of this Todd, what could I possibly get you as a present?"

"Oh, just the occasional dollar draft at The Goal Crease will suffice."

65

Despite Todd's nuptials, things pretty much remained the same, now Todd was really a man of leisure and could do anything he wanted.

Joe is driving Todd back from another day at the beach. They stayed a little later than usual, and both felt energized. Todd did not want the day to end quite yet, Joe was tired but was always game for fun. It was ladies' night at a place called The Ranch. Todd heard that the women there were plentiful, and who could miss out with those cowgirls, he thought? He reached out to a few other guys and they were game. The place was a western themed place, not a beach bar or tiki that Joe was used to frequenting. Joe was excited to check it out and did not have a change of clothes.

Rick meets them at the door, Rick dressed in appropriate wear for this venue.

"Are you sure you want to go in, Joe? I think they have a dress code."

Joe is eager but reluctant to go in. "What, everything down here is casual dress, Rick, you of all people should know that."

Rick gives him the once over, shaking his head and laughing. "Yeah, Joe but that floral pattern swimsuit that you've been wearing all day with that striped shirt does not seem to fit the motif of this place."

Joe is indignant and wants to enter anyway. "What, it has a collar, it is classy enough for this cow joint, I should blend in fine. Besides, I didn't even want to come in here, you're lucky I even came along. I am definitely not into country and western; line dancing is the stupidest way to dance."

"Yeah Joe, your way of dancing is way better than that, you are a regular Gene Kelly."

"Who, Rick? Did he invent the line dancing or whatever, because I know I'd never take credit for that."

"Well, Joe this is called The Ranch and some of the cutest girls and women come here to line dance. I know you like pretty chicks, and they have one of the largest bars in the region that serves your favorite, Budweiser."

"Well, I have to admit, it looks ok out there sight wise and the chicks seem kind of hot, but that doesn't look like the type of dancing I like to do."

"True, Joe, I have seen how you dance, looks like a Mexican jumping bean, no one dances like you, trust me."

"Everyone has a big hat on their heads, what's up with that?"

"Those are called Stetsons, partner."

"Well, you'll never catch me wearing those stupid hats."

They decide to go in and the first thing they see is a spatial, open dance floor with a long bar that the bartenders can slide drinks along, like the bars portrayed in those old western movies Joe used to watch as a kid.

Joe steps up to the bar and orders a Bud from the gorgeous bartender. She is wearing the standard cowgirl outfit, plaid shirt, tight jeans, and a black cowboy hat with tassels on it. Joe deliberately walks five paces to see if she can do the fancy move of sliding the beer to him.

Just then, a couple of hotties walk by drawing Joe's undivided attention. He stares at them as they walk by and his beer slides by him and falls off the edge of the bar.

Rick yells at Joe to pay attention, that it is a waste of perfectly good beer, but he orders another one for Joe.

Now the group of guys have assembled, and they are watching the action on the dance floor when one of them looks over at a few folks trying their bull riding skills on a mechanical bull.

Jeremiah quips and says he would bet any of them that he could last longer on it than everyone else.

Joe and Patrick say they want no part of it. Rick says he is game, confident that his outfit and aura gives him an advantage, and Todd decides to give it a shot even though he complains that his groin area was still chafed from their day at the beach. They agree to put up $10 each and Todd agrees to go first.

He stays on the bull for a fairly long time, it seems like it anyway, reaching an impressive 42 seconds, finally being unceremoniously dumped when the speed of the machine bull changes to faster. Joe chides Todd for his effort.

Jeremiah laughs at Todd, and says" You lightweight, watch how a real man rides a bull."

Jeremiah's confidence soon deflates when he puts the coins in the bull to start it up, he seats himself firmly on the mount, and literally, after the first jerking motion, he abruptly falls off the side of it, holding on to it with one arm but his feet touch the ground, so his ride to glory is over immediately.

He slinks off, his face as red as a beet and no one says a word.

Finally, Rick tells everybody to clear the space. He jumps up on the seat. The bull motion starts slowly at first and Rick has no problem hanging on, then it speeds up and the bucking motion increases. At this point, Rick grabs onto the attached handle and is riding it like a pro. He starts whooping and gets confident as he holds on with just one hand, waving his cowboy hat to everybody as the speed and frequency of bucking increases. He stays on so long; an employee comes over and manually turns the machine off.

Rick gets off the bull, and walks woozily over to Jeremiah, hands out, as Jeremiah hands him his $10 bill and says, "You got lucky."

Rick remarks, "I guess my times at Coochie Ha Has has finally paid some dividends."

Joe, who has the attention span of a gnat sometimes is now looking at the cute female line dancers and decides he could easily do it, but he is conscious of his dress and wants to impress the cowgirls. Rick approaches the pretty bartender and offers the $10 he just won to her if she would let Joe use her hat. She reluctantly hands it over as she slips the cash in her pocket.

Joe suddenly gets enthusiastic and energized now that he finally looks like a cowboy. The floor is at least a few hundred feet long and wide, it almost looks like it used to be a roller-skating rink at one time. There is an open area behind him where there are assembled lines of girls and women and a few guys doing traditional line dance steps, all in a nice uniform order.

A song comes on that Joe recognizes and he starts to get into it, and now starts acting like he is riding a bull as he hops up and down, starting to wave his hat as he starts running, bouncing and hopping from one end of the floor to the other end. The others are in complete shock, mouths dropping, most of the partic-ipants on the the floor fleeing to give Joe room to do his freestyle line dancing, all the while, the entire dance floor opens up for him. Everybody is pointing at Joe, some taking their phones out to video this travesty, watching this apparent lunatic acting like he is riding a bucking bronco, pointing at everyone as he runs along the railing on the long side of the floor.

Joe's group of friends sit stunned in silence as Joe continues his routine. The song is an extended version and Joe continues at the frenetic pace he started this dance. The song comes to a merciful end, the place is completely quiet when Joe comes off the dance floor, a smattering of claps and hoots in the background.

Joe approaches his friends. "How did you like my interpretation of line dancing?"

They are speechless, then Todd speaks for the group. "I can honestly say I have never seen anything like it." They all start laughing hysterically and pat Joe on the back.

Rick asks for the hat to return it to the bartender. The bartender refuses his gesture to return it to her, she does not want it back after that incident.

Finally, one of the bouncers comes over laughing and says, "Sir, some of the others complained about how you ruined their night, and they'd like you to leave and that you are a disgrace to line dancing everywhere. Personally, I think you should stay, but a lot of folks left in disgust already. That, and he says how Joe appears to be intoxicated.

Rick speaks back to the bouncer. "He's not that drunk yet, that's the way he usually is, lighten up on him, buddy."

Joe is incensed at the others' intolerance of his dancing. "Fuck them, Rick, if they don't know the art of dancing when they see it, that was freestyle form. Don't these guys appreciate the spontaneity and creativity of my dancing?"

"I've said it before, Joe, you sure know how to clear a room, or in this case, a 50 yard dance floor, good job, either way, you have to go. The bartender said to keep the hat as a memento of your last time here."

Joe fishes in his pockets. "Ok, Rick, truth is, I did not really appreciate this place anyway, now where did I put my keys, damn."

The night was not over for Joe. While they were inside, he promised to drop his brother and Patrick off afterwards. Joe is frantically searching for his keys. Maybe they fell out of his pocket while he was dancing, maybe he left them on the bar or in the restroom. He must humble himself as he enters back into the place that just kicked him out. He goes inside and asks if anyone has seen his keys, and no one claims they have, so Joe goes back to his minivan only to discover that it was running, that he left the keys in the ignition this whole time. The car was not running anymore as it ran out of gas. He panics for a second but then remembers he has AAA and calls to get the situation resolved. It is late and the wait time is over an hour.

He and his brother and Patrick look around and see a small place that still looks open, so they head over for a few beers while they wait for the tow truck driver, might as well make the most of the situation.

66

They grow the fish bigger and meaner in the Gulf than they do back home in the Great Lakes. Jeremiah had been assigned another unrelated job, but still knew that time was ticking on this current one involving his current passenger, probably still hungover from a night out, snoring, unusually loud, Joe who was snuggled up against his shoulder. He should just go to a cliff somewhere and open the door and push Joe out. The problem is, there are no mountains in Florida to speak of. Maybe an opportunity would present itself out on the open seas?

Finally, after almost a full hour in the car and two pit stops, Jeremiah and Joe arrive at the dock. They are a few minutes late for the scheduled departure and while Joe goes to the bathroom to relieve himself, Jeremiah insists that the boat waits for his friend.

Jeremiah makes an offer they can't refuse so they wait almost 15 minutes until Joe finally gets on the boat. "Gee, Jeremy, I feel like I never see you around much anymore, glad you could come out on the 'Frolicking Fish Tour' boat, although it looks eerily similar to one that we took on that disastrous pirate adventure where Rick sank it by accident."

"Yeah, good times, Joe, good times. Those people onboard still remember me making them walk the gang plank, reminds me of those times in Aruba, uh, never mind, John. "

"You'd think you knew my name well by now, Jer, my name is plastered everywhere down on the beach, so I'm starting to find places off the beach that are not aware of my escapades. Well, I am glad I found the discount coupon for this tour, too, in the local tourist coupon magazine, Jer."

"Good thing, too, Joe, because I have some time off between jobs, kind of surprised that you get the free admission and I had to pay full price but at least you made up for it by bringing those famous manmosa beverages I like."

"It does seem like you forget things every time you go away on these jobs, though."

"Let's just go, Joe, and relax and catch some fish on the boat, at least I won't have to bait your hook all the time like I do all the time when we fish."

The boat finally pulls out of the dock pretty late, some of the other passengers grumbling about the wait, to make its way to the Gulf. It picks up speed, but it seems like it is not going anywhere.

After a while, it's just open water, and the shoreline disappears, Joe panics a bit. "Why's it taking so long to get out where the fish are, Jer? I don't get it, why are the fish that far away?"

"Just relax and enjoy the trip, Joe, good thing we brought that cooler of manmosas."

The boat is approaching its first stop to anchor down and let the eager inexperienced want to be fishers drop their lines and take selfies of themselves showing how much fun they are supposedly having. Most of the group on this current expedition are overweight whale white visitors from Minnesota on winter break to get a suntan to make themselves look better.

The overused loud, crackly PA comes over the speakers, the captain's voice inaudible. "Ok, ladies and gentlemen and that idiot in the floral pattern swimsuit and striped shirt, we have reached our destination, our pretend mates that act as doubles on the Pirate Cruise will hook your bait, pull your catch off the hook, and get you beers for a charge, we have to announce that for our esteemed and obnoxious guest onboard."

Jeremiah shakes his head in disgust, he did not need this unwanted attention on this usually lightly attended excursion. "You are always so noticeable, honestly, Joe, I am glad I don't have to be discreet on this boat or anything."

The crew efficiently helps its passengers bait their hooks and even casts the lines for some and fetch a drink for some of the thirsty fishermen. Joe notices a few other customers having some luck landing fish, sees the crew even taking the fish off their hooks.

All this for $179 each for this otherwise cheap experience. One of the passengers, though, was smart enough, or cheap enough, to take advantage of the miniscule coupon in the little cheesy coupon book placed in all the little mailbox things down along the beach.

"Now this is service, Jer, isn't it, all I do is sit back, wait till a fish bites, yank it up and let everyone else do the rest. I hope I catch one of those big 'Jewfish'."

"Joe, they are not called Jewfish anymore they are called Goliath Groupers now."

"Huh, what, are you kidding me? Are we that sensitive to name calling that we can't call those huge fish with hook nosed snouts, Jewfish? I suppose we won't be able to call the Washington Redskins, the Redskins anymore, either?"

Jeremiah is just about to say something when a sudden, strong jerk on Joe's pole interrupts him. Joe is almost pulled over the side by the motion and he grabs at anything he can hold. "Oh wait, I think I got something, oh man, whatever it is huge, my arms are getting sore from pulling on it, can you grab this pole, Jer, I got to use the potty."

Joe immediately puts the reel in Jeremiah's hand before Jeremiah could react and runs off to use the bathroom. Joe is gone for over 10 minutes and Jeremiah is struggling but holds his own with this catch. Jeremiah looks over disgustedly at Joe but is also enjoying this challenge to see what's on the other side of this line. "You only were only pulling about a minute, Joe."

"How long have you been at it, Jer, even you, a big strapping field lacrosse goalie can't even pull it up, he's a fighter, I tell you."

Jeremiah makes one huge yank and closes his eyes in anticipation of finally reeling in this monster fish. It finally breaks the surface and lands on the deck of the boat. Joe is in mid-sentence when the action comes to a grinding halt. "Wait, it looks like you are getting it in, keep yanking, keep pulling, Jer, almost there. What the fuck is it, is it a dolphin, holy shit it looks like a man, oh my God!"

Some of the passengers are beyond horrified and run for cover so as not to see this spectacle, some take their phones out to get pictures, everyone is stunned by this sudden turn of events.

Jeremiah is not as surprised as the others when he takes a look at the victim. "How the fuck did he get out here, I thought I buried him out by Galveston."

Joe is close by and hears Jeremiah's nonchalant comment. "What did you say, Jer?"

"Oh, just that the currents usually go west, not east. I heard once that most bodies end up over by Mexico."

"How would you know that fact, Jer?"

"I am a curious kind of guy, that's all, I had to study it in college once as part of marine biology."

The crew immediately covers the body with a tarp and downplays the incident quickly and decisively. They don't want this incident to ruin their business. Lord knows it's been an expensive year, what with the Pirate ship sinking and resulting lawsuits. The captain decides to end the fishing part of the tour and declare the winner of the biggest fish caught was Joe because he originally hooked the now decomposing body. While no one is looking, one of the crew quietly dispatches the tarp over the side, and no one is the wiser.

Jeremiah still thinks he should have won the prize for the biggest catch of the day because it was him that reeled it in, not loser Joe. The captain, after a few minutes of deliberation on the issues, decides that Joe should win because he is less intelligent and naïve and won't be smart enough or sober enough to realize what happened.

Joe is celebrating his fortune when he spots Jeremiah on his phone in a secretive manner. "Why are you on your phone, Jer, can you even get service out here? Who did you have to call?"

"I forgot it was my mom's birthday and wanted to wish her a happy birthday, just because you aren't close to your family doesn't mean I ain't."

This whole grisly incident including the trip out from the dock took slightly more than half an hour and the boat is headed in the direction of the dock already and even Joe, as inexperienced as he is in nautical matters notices it. "Looks like we are turning around and heading back to shore, we were only out here a half hour, what a gyp, I am gonna ask for a refund, this sucks."

"You didn't even pay, Joe, you came on a groupon and made me pay my whole fare, whatever." Jeremiah tosses his plastic cup of manmosa overboard.

"Still, Jer, I count as a participant, a winning one at that. I am deserving of a refund."

Just then a very loud, obnoxious oversized speed boat pulls up alongside the idling deep sea charter boat. Joe is distracted by dolphins flipping in the water, until he turns around and sees Jeremiah scurrying off the charter boat and climbing a rope to the waiting speedboat. "Why is that high powered speedboat approaching on the right? Jer, where you going?"

"I forgot I left cookies in the oven, Joe, these are my friends that offered to take me back to my place so I could turn off the oven. Catch you at the Goal Crease later."

Joe screams loudly back at Jeremiah as he watches him speed away. "Well, at least I had the biggest catch of the day and won the trophy, too bad it wasn't a keeper."

67

The syndicate was in contact with Jeremiah. He wanted to run away and hide, told them he finished the job, end of story, then he could move on to the next hopefully more lucrative job. The grand jury was being called in and even though Joe was still not there, it was only a matter of time. Joe was still walking and breathing, he even knew where Joe was this very instant. It wasn't so much that Joe's end of the equation was not resolved yet, but the fact that Jeremiah had negotiated his full fee beforehand, an occurrence that usually never occurs in hit dom world. Jeremiah knew the group was desperate to tie up loose ends. The real dilemma was that Jeremiah was having so much fun, and blowing through so much money that he did not have the available funds to cover his next month's expenses. 'Oh, move to Florida, Jeremiah it's cheaper there', my ass, he thought. The rents kept going up drastically, even after the Hurricanes, and happy hours that once were $0.99 drafts and $5 wings doubled or tripled at the very least in the last year.

Back to matter at hand, as much as Jeremiah actually liked Joe for his adventurous, free spirit attitude and willingness to always join in whatever crazy antics and activities the game concocted, the stark reality was Joe had to go, Jeremiah needed another payday. Rick was conveniently out of town, probably treating some whore dujour at some fancy place in Boca or something, and he asked Joe in front of him to stop over and check the place and reset the traps for him.

Rick had a well-kept garden and bird sanctuary that he worked hard to keep in pristine shape, it was his pride and joy, even Jeremiah knew that. Joe agreed to run over to Rick's place between the late morning happy hours at the beach, and the late afternoon happy hour at the Goal Crease.

Jeremiah knew Joe would be on his own to take care of the chores, so he planned on surprising Joe face to face in Rick's utopian garden and bird sanctuary, to send Joe to his own sort of eutopia. Jeremiah at least had to face Joe man to man and tell him he enjoyed all the laughs over the last few months, but business was business. He had hoped Joe would not cry and quiver and beg for his life, or that he, Joe, would not show the surprise and disappointment at that final stage of life removal that Jeremiah had experienced so many times before. He maybe got a little too personal this job. He would wait at the back corner of Rick's house, Joe would walk up to unload and reset the trap and Jeremiah would do 'the dirty deed', slip out of town and never be seen again.

All was going as planned. Jeremiah pulled up to the street, left his car down the block and sauntered to Rick's, whistling as he went. He brought his special gun, it was efficient and got the job done neat and clean, no mess. As Jeremiah walked along the side of the house, he encountered something new and different than what he saw the last time he was at Rick's a couple months back. There was an easy opening gate leading to his backyard, Jeremiah opened the gate quietly and took a few steps.

All of a sudden, the sound of automatic clicking occurred. Jeremiah reached back to let himself out, but the gate locked, only giving one way to proceed. 'What the fuck', Jeremiah thought. Who puts a maze-like gate in their backyard?

He turned another corner and came to another gate. Now Jeremiah was getting frustrated and pissed. He had hoped to walk into an open backyard, take care of business at hand, no fuss, no muss. He wasn't thinking as he kept walking when another series of clicking happened and now, he was doubly locked into the stupid maze. He tried to turn back around but the gate would not give so he kept moving on.

Jeremiah was getting so aggravated, he came to the idea that when he got through this stupid maze, he would not only strangle Joe but Rick too. He now encounters a small solid fence, and he starts to scale it when he slips on the top and slides into a large metallic container with rounded sides. Slipping enough that he could not hoist himself out of this strangely boxlike container with shiny slippery sides.

Then the top was closing off the sun from outside as a flat lid started sliding over the once open top. It was starting to get dark and suffocating. Jeremiah suddenly realizes he is now caught in what seems to be a trash compactor device and there is no way to escape. He is pissed at himself for the fact that he let down his guard, and worse yet, seems to have been outsmarted by a lesser intellectual guy, and that Joe would skip happily along as though nothing phases him. Jeremiah screams, "I hope everything you love dies in your arms, you fucker!"

Just then, the compactor reaches the bottom of the container crushing everything in it.

Everything is peaceful and quiet at Rick's place. Joe came and went that night, checked the trap Rick had set for the squirrels and rodents, fed the birds, and barely noticed that Rick had a dumpster-like container sitting in the backyard.

Joe thought to himself, that wasn't there the last time, but Joe being the oblivious, happy go lucky kind of guy he is, hurriedly did the chores to get to the Goal Crease to get his seat and have $1 Bud drafts.

A few days later, Joe and Rick are sitting in front of Rick's place when a large private company dump truck empties the dumpster from Rick's backyard, the truck toots its horn when they are done, and Rick smiles and waves to them.

"Gee Rick I haven't heard or seen anything of Jeremiah the past few days, have you heard anything from him?"

"No, Joe I haven't he's probably off crushing some unsuspecting woman's heart or something."

"Oh", Joe says as he scratches his chin. "So, I meant to ask you, Rick what do you usually catch in those traps anyway?"

"Eh, mostly rats Joe, mostly rats".

68

Joe is having a dream, a dream about him jumping into the Blue Hole in Jamaica. It is a waterfall where you climb up about 20 feet and plunge into the rushing water. Joe has the sensation of plunging deep into the water and he struggles to get to the top where he can breathe. He flails and panics as he attempts to break the surface and breathe. He suddenly bolts upright, alert, and aware of his surroundings. Wait a minute he thinks, 'where is my little clock radio on the side of my bed, the window that lets in light in the morning and my little makeshift table I used to eat at and use my laptop'? He surveys his surroundings. The bed is not at ground level. This room is clean and sterile, almost clinical with four white walls and a bed higher in the middle of the room. Wait, is that a machine next to the bed with digital numbers and little flashy lights? There are wires and tubes everywhere.

"Where am I?"

"Joe, Joe, come in Joe, calling Joe."

Joe is befuddled and confused looking around the room. "Huh, whuh?"

"It's me Joel, your buddy. Can you hear me, Joe? Are you Ok?"

Joe is immediately snapped back to the present and asks where he is. A strange man with a white coat, gray slacks and a name tag walks up to Joe's side of the bed. He announces that he is Dr. Raji Shiv, head neurologist at Buffalo General Hospital. He tells Joe, "You are lucky to be alive, young man. You had a very serious accident and suffered a traumatic brain injury. You've been in a coma for over a week. Your ex-wife even had a priest administer Last Rites to you."

Joel pipes up, "Yeah, she even wanted to pull the plug on you. But I wouldn't let them. I made them keep you on life support because I knew you'd hang on to annoy everyone as long as you could."

The doctor speaks up, "Do you know who you are?"

Joe speaks up surely and without hesitation, "Yes, I'm Joe, Joe from Buffalo."

The doctor raises his eyebrows skeptically and asks, "Do you know where you live Joe?"

"I was staying at my buddy Joel's basement, but I moved to Florida. I was living with David in Fort Myers. Where's Todd, Rick, and Jer?"

Dr. Shiv continues his questioning as he shines his penlight into Joe's eyes. "Do you know what day it is today?"

"Sure, it's January 10th, right?"

"No, today is January 17 and you have been in a coma for a week."

Joe's badly damaged head is swirling now, and he is having difficulty comprehending what he has just heard. "Joel, Joel, you've got to believe me. I lived in Fort Myers for a few years. I met some great friends, and we did a lot of fun things. I even remember getting into trouble for a lot of dumb things, at least I thought they were. Who gets thrown out of a bar for bad karaoke singing? The beach was so beautiful and there was a place called the Goal Crease in Fort Myers. They had $1 Bud drafts. I would go there practically every night, people knew who I was, 'Joe, Joe from Buffalo'." Joe is becoming more and more agitated as he tells them, "I met a group of guys, and we went and did stuff all the time. Beaches, happy hours, golfing, boats, parties, I swear I was there, Joel. I even met chicks, lots of chicks, and hooked up with Sarah etc. etc." He continues talking louder and more insistent, "Joel, I heard you died while I was in Florida. I left your place in January to get away from the snow and this weather, and an ex that was always up my ass."

"Well Joe, part of that is true, you still have an ex. I just saw her in the elevator. She told me she still needs her payments on the first or she's going to call her lawyer and have your income garnished. As for your fantasy or dream life you are telling me about, you were never in Florida at beaches, tiki bars or any of that. You were in a sleep-like state. You didn't make it further than a mile from here. You never made it to the interstate. You were in a devastating car crash, and we didn't think you were gonna make it."

Doctor Shiv presses on with his questions. "Do you remember anything about the night of the accident?"

"No, I don't even remember going to bed the night before. I do remember the Sabres lost the game. Is this real? Are you guys playing a sick prank on me?"

"No, afraid not. From what we learned, you were in a serious crash and were found convulsing on the front passenger seat. You had internal brain trauma, and your right frontal lobe was crushed. You have been hospitalized for a week and did not move once." With that pronouncement, Dr. Shiv exits the room, leaving the confused brain injured patient alone with his friend.

"I'm telling you Joel, as God is my witness, I have vivid details of places. I even remember a place called the Ranch where I danced and scared the women off the dance floor. I remember fishing on a bridge in Pine Island and lots of happy hours at the beach. I know I was there!"

Just then, another friend, Paul, enters the room. "Hey Joe, it's me Paul, do you remember me?"

"Of course, I do silly. You made fun of my decision to go to Florida. Why?"

Paul is concerned about his disillusioned friend. But being a betting man, he is thinking about parlaying this situation into a money-making proposition. "Well, if what you said really happened, can you tell me who won the Super Bowl next season? If you were there for years, then you know some stuff in the future we can make money on."

"No, I don't remember who won the game or whatever, but I swear I was there, it seemed so real. I got to have something to prove I was there. No one believes me. This is just like how I was getting into trouble all the time down there. There must be a record or something. Wait! They know me at Goal Crease, get ahold of them, Joel. Ask for Alex or Marissa, the bartenders. No, no, ask if they saw Todd there today."

"Ok Joe, we will call there." Joel pulls out his cell phone to look up the Goal Crease in Fort Myers Florida. Joel shakes his head in sympathy. "Seems like there are no places listed with that name, little buddy. Are you sure you were there? There's the Quarterback Club, The Dugout, The Courtside, but no place called Goal Crease, sorry."

His friends exchange looks. "You need to get some rest Joe. Maybe you just imagined a life there, maybe you just wanted something different than what you have here. I don't know what to tell you."

Joe feels like he is living a Rip Van Winkle story. He wakes up after 20 years and the world changed, or did it? It is too soon to look in a mirror. If this is real, he cannot imagine how disfigured he must be and how his face must be contorted and bruised.

Life is comprised of different experiences, some real, some imagined, some shared with others, some alone but ultimately it is you that is at the center of those experiences. May you take the best option for yourself and live your dreams to the fullest extent possible.

Made in the USA
Monee, IL
03 November 2023

45670203R00197